"You didn't just *accidentally* slip into this damn negligee."

Ryan sounded angry, and Sunny twisted in his threatening grip. "Of course not. But I—"

"But nothing." His hands moved from her lace-covered shoulders to her bare upper arms. "I want you too damn much to pretend not to notice."

Breathlessly, she whispered, "You do?"

Ryan swallowed a groan. Her gaze had gone all soft and sultry. Was she taunting him? "You know I do."

Sunny parted the lacy edges of her gown to reveal her full, high breasts. Ryan's breathing, his heartbeat, his universe stilled.

"This is no accident, either," she whispered.

Ryan searched her tempestuous green eyes. "It better not be, Sunny," he uttered hoarsely, "because I'm not going to stop."

Donna Sterling has been a proofreader, a
waitress, a real estate agent, a school librarian, a
shrimper…but her secret passion was romance,
her secret vice daydreaming. When she
discovered Harlequin she realized she could put
the two together and have yet another career—
this time as an award-winning author.
Something Old, Something New is Donna's
first published novel, but her next Temptation
story is already in the works.

Married, with two young sons, two grown
stepsons and a pet iguana, she lives in a log cabin
in northeast Georgia where, as Donna says, she
"daydreams to her heart's content."

To Anne Bushyhead, Ann White and Gin Ellis for
their in-depth critiques and support.
To my grandmothers, who passed on to me a
love of storytelling.
To my mother, my guiding light, who nurtured
my love of the written word.
To my father, my pillar, who endowed me with the self-
confidence I needed to keep on trying.
To my husband, my inspiration, who taught me the
essence of romance.
To my sons, the coolest of the cool, who continually
gladden my heart.
And to Brenda Chin, the woman who made
my dream come true.
I love you all.

Donna Sterling
SOMETHING OLD, SOMETHING NEW

Harlequin Books

TORONTO • NEW YORK • LONDON
AMSTERDAM • PARIS • SYDNEY • HAMBURG
STOCKHOLM • ATHENS • TOKYO • MILAN
MADRID • WARSAW • BUDAPEST • AUCKLAND

ISBN 0-373-25686-8

SOMETHING OLD, SOMETHING NEW

Copyright © 1996 by Donna Fejes.

1

RYAN ALEXANDER STARED at the envelope his secretary had placed on his desk. Although the return address did not include a name, he knew who had sent it. An almost-forgotten tension tightened his muscles.

The handwriting was Sunny's.

His first impulse was to throw the letter away unopened. To leave the past where it belonged—safely buried. But curiosity overcame his reluctance. He slit open the envelope.

A simple sketch on the front of the folded stationery caught his attention. Pencil strokes portrayed a little girl in pigtails, her right eye closed in a wink. A wink without a smile.

Which, at one time, had meant "something's up." Something new and unfailingly interesting.

They'd been kids then, left to run wild every summer at Windsong Place. Sunny had been the housekeeper's granddaughter; he, the man of the house—in his father's absence, of course. Those had been the innocent years.

Ryan gripped the paper tighter. The innocence had ended the summer he returned from his junior year in college to find his childhood pal gone, and in her place, a dream. A dewy-skinned, bright-eyed dream that made his blood simmer and his rational thought evaporate like steam.

By autumn, they had married. In winter, she had left him.

Dropping the unread letter onto his desk, Ryan pushed his leather chair back and paced across his Manhattan penthouse office, his hands in the pockets of his Italian suit.

Their involvement had been a mistake. A hormonal thing. Unchecked teenage passion. They married to give their unborn baby a secure family life—something neither of them had had. But their plans ended with a miscarriage. In her grief, Sunny had left him.

Ryan clearly understood why. The reason for their marriage had no longer existed. He hadn't tried to stop her. Hadn't seen any justification for her to stay.

His fists clenched within his pockets.

Thoughts of her always brought back disturbing memories. His father had disinherited him because of their marriage. And though Ryan didn't believe so, the mere possibility that his loss of fortune had influenced her decision to leave taunted him.

His father had taken great pains to convince him of it, but Ryan refused to believe he had misjudged her that drastically.

Regardless of her motive for leaving, Sunny and he had parted friends. She sent him Christmas cards every year. He kept her name on his corporate card-mailing list tended by his secretary. Yes, indeed, Ryan assured himself, Sunny and he were friends. Nothing more, nothing less. Ten years and dozens of romantic liaisons had nearly erased the memory of her face.

Returning to his desk, he unfolded the note.

Ryan,
Need to talk to you about Windsong Place. I'd like to move back there. Let's work out a deal. Call me.
                                                        Sunny

Ryan frowned. She wanted to move back to Windsong Place?

Was she the one bidding against him to buy it? Perhaps the rival bidder wasn't his father, as Ryan had assumed when he heard that "another Alexander" had also put in a bid for the North Carolina mountaintop mansion.

Windsong Place. It had been his late mother's ancestral home, where Ryan was born and raised. By all rights, he should have inherited it. But his father had sold the house in a fit of rage when he learned Ryan had married Sunny.

How could Sunny possibly afford to buy it even as a franchise?

Suddenly, suspicion flashed through him like cold air on a sore tooth, and the ugliest explanation reared its head. *Had she accepted the payoff his father offered her to leave him?* No. Ryan couldn't, wouldn't, believe it. Sunny hadn't married him for money, or left him because he'd lost it.

But a cynical inner voice persisted: if she *was* the rival bidder, where else would she have come up with that much cash? According to her last Christmas card, she now managed a small Atlanta hotel. Not much chance of a million-dollar gain there.

Unless she'd hit some lottery. With Sunny's luck, Ryan seriously doubted it.

Which left very few other possibilities.

Cursing, Ryan crumpled the note. He had to know. He'd do more than call her. He'd break a rule he had kept faithfully for ten long years. He'd pay Sunny a visit.

BY THE NEXT MORNING—a bright and breezy Thursday in May—Ryan had thoroughly prepared himself to face the discovery that Sunny had indeed taken his father's bribe to leave him.

In a sullen mood, he flew from New York to Atlanta, then guided the sleek, powerful sports car he'd rented down tree-canopied boulevards toward the hotel she managed. If she was the "other Alexander" bidding against him for control of Windsong Place, he'd quickly disillusion her about her chances of buying it.

Then he'd rent a Harley-Davidson—buy one, if he had to—and head out toward the north Georgia mountains. Ride a few high ridges. Maybe climb a few rocks. His muscles ached for strenuous exercise; his mind craved a thrill. Something gut level. Something dangerous. Anything drastic enough to hold the emptiness at bay.

It haunted him, the emptiness, creeping in from all sides when least expected. His career had once helped to fend it off, but lately the corporate winnings seemed too easy, the satisfaction, too brief. Much like his romantic liasons, if they could be called that.

His car glided to a halt in front of the quaint, tree-shaded hotel near Emory University. Ryan's tension grew. He hadn't seen Sunny since their divorce. He wondered how much she had changed. Not that he cared one way or another. He was no longer a green kid, and she was no longer a teenage beauty.

As he shut the car door, a slender, fair-haired girl wheeled past him on a gold ten-speed bicycle into the hotel parking lot. No, not a girl. A woman.

Ryan leaned back against the car and watched her dismount from the bike. She walked it to the side of the building and parked it behind a white latticework wall. When she reemerged, he caught a clear view of her. *Sunny.*

She wore faded jeans and a yellow T-shirt, the same kind of clothes she'd always worn. Her hair was shorter than it had been; chin-length, with curls that glistened and bounced. Her fair skin radiated its usual healthy glow. The curves of her slim figure seemed more rounded than he remembered.

She was attractive. He had to give her that. The kind of woman who would catch any man's eye. Except his. She wouldn't catch his, ever again.

As she approached the front door of the hotel, she noticed him standing there beside his car and did a quick double take. Like a deer mesmerized by oncoming headlights, she stood frozen, staring at him.

She was appealing, yes. But the sight of her had *not* stopped his heart, or interfered with his breathing. Her presence had not affected him in any way. He exhaled his pent-up breath in relief. He was safe. In the clear. On solid ground.

But then she smiled.

DON'T JUST STAND HERE like a numbskull, Sunny told herself. *Say something. Something intelligent and warm and welcoming.* But her mind was filled with the sight of him, looking even more devastatingly handsome than he had in her dreams.

His ebony hair gleamed in the same wind-blown waves around his suntanned face—an arresting, *vital* face, although time had etched a subtle austerity into its lean ruggedness. His jaw was still strong and square, the vertical cleft in his chin well-defined. And the pure male power emanating from him still raised goose bumps on her arms and made her legs go weak.

Okay, try for something coherent. She managed a breathless "Ryan!"

Good, she thought. *Now do something. Pretend you have some sense.* He wasn't helping. He hadn't uttered a word. His gray eyes regarded her steadily, giving no clue to his thoughts.

Oh, God, she thought, *I must look a wreck.* Old clothes, no makeup. She wished she could sink down through the gravel. But she couldn't. *Might as well face the music and dance.* She jolted herself into action, smiling with delight, letting her joy at seeing him bubble to the surface.

He watched her approach with a look of wariness.

As she reached him, fully intending to hug him, he smiled a cool, businesslike smile and extended his hand. "Sunny," he murmured. His voice, deep and naturally hoarse, retained a subtle southern drawl, almost imperceptible now from years of travel, but enough to lend a soft sensuality.

A spiral of warmth curled through her. She had forgotten the effect of his voice.

She hesitated, thrown off stride. Perhaps he was right. A handshake might be better. She accepted his outstretched hand with professional aplomb.

But when his warm, strong hand clasped hers, a tender emotion engulfed her. How she had missed him! He had been an ache in a secret part of her heart for far too long. She smiled at him through a teary mist.

"Ry," she whispered.

Their handclasp tightened. Her smile wavered beneath his stare. And a sensual energy pulsed through her—dark, primitive, intensely erotic. It warmed her from the inside out, until she was sure the heat radiated from her skin like sunbeams. Shaken, she broke away from his touch.

So, her memory hadn't exaggerated. And her hope had been in vain. She was no stronger now against his potent sexuality than she had been ten years ago.

But she was wiser now, she reminded herself. Much wiser.

Struggling for a breath, Sunny offered a silent prayer of thanks that she hadn't hugged him. How would she ever have composed herself afterward? She blurted the first inane greeting that sprang to her lips. "Long time no see."

He nodded, cool and self-assured, as he thrust his hands into the pockets of his fashionable dove-gray trousers. He seemed taller than she remembered and his shoulders looked broader beneath an expensive charcoal blazer and blue silk shirt. She remembered marveling at the hardness of those shoulders, those biceps, running her fingertips over every muscle....

Quickly she drew her gaze away from his shoulders. *Friends, Sunny!* she warned herself silently. *Only friends.*

She channeled her nervousness into scolding. "Darn you, Ryan, why didn't you let me know you were coming? I would've liked to impress you with my youthful face," she said with a laugh, "but I didn't have time to put it on this morning."

His smoky, veiled gaze did not lighten. "Am I supposed to say you're beautiful as you are?"

Taken aback, she stood in embarrassed silence. Had he meant that to be funny? She hoped so. "I never knew you to tell pretty lies before." She tried another tentative grin. "But hey, it's not too late to start."

"Okay. It's good to see you again, Sunny."

Was he implying it wasn't? "At least your timing's good. Today's my day off. We'll have time to talk."

"We won't need much time."

Sunny wondered what on earth he could possibly be miffed about. She hadn't seen him in ten years! Determined to break through his bewildering coolness, she invited him into her private efficiency apartment for coffee.

For a moment, she thought he'd refuse. But after a short hesitation, he followed her into the hotel lobby, past the front desk, down the blue-carpeted corridor to her door.

Damn her, Ryan cursed silently. *Damn her for her easy friendliness.* Here he was, shell-shocked from the feel of her palm against his. And she had been about to hug him. Hug him, for God's sake. Like a relative at a family reunion.

Now she was smiling at him in the same happy way she had when they were kids. Except she carried herself with a new confidence, a quiet authority. As if she could easily handle any problem life might throw at her, while he was having trouble just looking at her.

As she unlocked her door, he wrested his gaze away. He'd been a damned fool over her once, going against his father's ultimatum: "Marry her, and I'll cut you off without a penny. You won't be my son."

Ryan had married her, anyway. Told his father to keep his damned money. And Sunny had left him.

She preceded him into a small living room that abounded with plants, sculptures—many of which he recognized as hers— paintings and knickknacks. One overstuffed armchair, an end table and a television comprised the living room furniture.

She led him beyond the living room to the far corner, which was separated by a long, low counter. The kitchen. "Have a seat." She waved to a chair at the diner-style, white-topped table. Ryan didn't sit. He wouldn't be staying that long.

As he leaned one hip against the kitchen counter, he surveyed the room. It looked more like an artist's studio than a kitchen, with easels, canvases, paints, brushes, tools, a small electric kiln, a drying rack and shelves stocked with art supplies. In one inconspicuous corner was a toaster and a microwave—her only means of cooking, he suspected. Ryan wasn't surprised. She never had been too good in the kitchen.

The bedroom was a different story.

Ryan clenched his teeth. Perhaps her long, intoxicating kisses hadn't been fueled by passion. Perhaps they'd been a part of a get-rich-quick scheme. Betrayal knifed through him as if it had happened yesterday, and he forgot his earlier decision that Sunny wasn't after his money.

As he struggled to suppress his anger, Sunny measured coffee into a filter for her coffeemaker. Ryan's eye was drawn beyond her by the half-finished oil painting on an easel. A Victorian mansion spread atop a mountain. Windsong Place.

"Well, what do you think?" she asked, turning in time to notice the direction of his gaze. "Does it look like home?" Her voice was soft and pleasing as a mountain breeze. He gritted his teeth even harder. "I painted it from the full-page ad in the real estate magazine." She cast him a shy smile. "My grandmother sent it to me—"

"Let's get to the point, Sunny," he interrupted brusquely. "What exactly is your interest in Windsong Place?"

"My interest?" Sunny set down the pitcher of water she had been pouring into the coffeemaker and gaped at him.

The question, and that cold, hurtful tone, pierced her. Didn't he know that his boyhood home would always hold a special place in her heart? It had been *her* home, too, for every summer of her childhood. The only constant home she'd known.

The one he had carried her into as his bride.

But she wouldn't think about that. Ever.

From the glacial look in Ryan's ice-gray eyes, she realized he wouldn't want to hear about her sentiments. She recognized his look. Something was eating away at him.

Since she had no idea what, she supposed the safest course was to tackle the subject from a strictly professional angle. In a brisk tone, she began, "I understand that the present owners are selling Windsong Place as a bed-and-breakfast inn."

"That's right." His voice was quiet; his gaze unaccountably menacing.

"Inns need managers." When she failed to respond to what Sunny considered a full explanation of her interest, she lifted her hands in a gesture. "Look around. What business have I been in for the past ten years? The hotel business. And I graduated from Emory University with a degree in management." When Ryan still hadn't commented, she explained in no uncertain terms, "I want to run the inn. Live there. Manage it."

Ryan's eyes darkened to storm-gray. "That's why you want Windsong Place—to further your career?"

Bewildered by his wording, Sunny frowned.

He didn't seem to notice. She sensed his anger gaining momentum, rather like a runaway freight train on a downhill track. Absolutely unstoppable.

"You know I'm bidding on Windsong Place," he said in clipped syllables.

"Well, yes, my grandmother told me you were."

"But you're not going to let that stop you, are you."

Sunny's bewilderment deepened. "Why should it?"

He drew nearer to her, a threat in every taut line of his muscled body. Gazing into his eyes, she imagined a freight train bearing down on her with all its deadly fury. "So, where did you get the money?"

Flustered by his nearness, puzzled by his anger and entirely baffled by his question, Sunny blinked. "What money?"

"Come on, now, Sunny. I find it hard to believe that you saved up enough to buy this franchise."

"Buy?" she repeated dumbly. Did he think *she* planned to buy Windsong Place? The idea was ludicrous. On her salary, she couldn't qualify for a two-bedroom condo. At least, not while she helped pay her grandmother's medical bills.

"Unless, of course," he continued coldly, advancing another menacing step, "you deposited a healthy sum into an interest-bearing account ten years ago."

Sunny stared at him, openmouthed. When she found her voice, she uttered, "Just what are you implying?"

Ryan insolently crossed his arms and didn't bother to answer. He didn't have to.

In angry disbelief, Sunny cried, "Your father told you about the bribe he offered me to leave you, didn't he."

"He mentioned it."

"Did he say that I accepted it?"

"He didn't have to say it, Sunny," he replied through clenched teeth, standing close enough to shake her. "How the hell else could you afford to buy into Windsong Place?"

Planting her hands on her hips, Sunny glared right back at him, her nose nearly touching his. "For being 'one of the most vital up-and-coming entrepreneurial forces in the nation,'" she said with scathing mockery, "you sure are stupid."

That set him back a step. The quote had come from a recent article in a business magazine. The insult, straight from the brat who used to stick her tongue out at him.

He realized that no one, but no one, had slighted him— by word, deed or action—in years. Since he'd made his first million, to be exact. He had been accorded only the highest respect. People fell all over themselves trying to win his approval. Yes, Mr. Alexander. Of course, Mr. Alexander. Anything you say, Mr. Alexander. Even the women he dated had been overly willing to please. Or at least, to impress.

But not Sunny. She had called him stupid. Stupid! She hadn't even bothered trying to be witty about it. If he hadn't been so angry with her, he might have laughed.

But he was angry with her. Damned angry. "Don't bid against me for Windsong Place," he advised her. "I'm willing to pay much more than you'll be able to afford."

Without a backward glance, he strode to the door and let it slam behind him. He heard her quick, light footsteps trailing him through the empty, carpeted corridor.

Before he reached the lobby, she called, "Don't flaunt your wealth in front of me. You should be thanking me for it."

He halted in his tracks, then slowly swung around to face her. "What the hell is that supposed to mean?"

After glaring at him, she shook her head. "Nothing. Never mind." She turned to go back into her apartment.

He retraced his steps down the corridor and grabbed her arm to keep her from going in. "Are you insinuating that my money came from my father after you left?"

"It's none of my business. I shouldn't have said anything about it." She jerked her arm away from his grasp. "But for your information, I wasn't planning to buy Windsong Place. I was stupid enough to hope *you* would."

Again, she had surprised him. She hoped *he'd* buy the mansion? "Why the hell would you want *me* to buy Windsong Place?"

With a glance around to be sure no one else was present, she whispered loudly, angrily, "So I could apply for the position of general manager."

"General manager?" he repeated.

"Of the inn," she specified, as if he wouldn't be capable of making the connection. "You know, live there and run it? I'm sure you don't plan to personally manage it."

"You want to work for me?" His mind reeled in confusion.

"You can forget that now. If you got down on your knees and begged me, I wouldn't work for you. As far as I'm concerned, Ryan Alexander," she said, her voice trembling as it always had when they fought, "you can go suck a lemon!"

And she shut the door in his face.

2

WITH AN ANGRY, DOWNWARD thrust of her knife, Sunny
sliced the block of moist, red earthenware clay into two
neat halves on her kitchen table. The blade embedded itself into the cutting board with a satisfying *thwunk*.

"And I thought we were friends," she muttered. Raising the knife, she chopped the clay again into two. How
naive she had been. She thought Ryan had been grateful
to her for divorcing him. Liberating him. Giving him back
his happiness.

But no—he had been resentful. Because he believed her
to be a gold digger. *Thwunk!* Another chunk of clay split
neatly apart beneath her merciless blade. Setting her knife
aside, she chose a wedge of clay to work with. Squeezing
it through her two fists—much like one might strangle an
insensitive, arrogant ex-husband—she found herself re-
living that morning's encounter.

The nerve of the man! After ten years he appeared out
of nowhere and flung accusations at her as if she were some
unscrupulous schemer.

Oh, the very thought infuriated her!

With a vengeance, she banged the hapless clay onto the
worktable and dug into its red moistness with the heels of
her hands. She might have been a fool for him once, but
she wouldn't be again. She'd forget about managing
Windsong Place, even though it would have been an answer to all of her problems. She'd find another way to ad-
vance her career; another way to live in the mountain

community near her ailing grandmother. The trick would be combining those two feats. But she'd find a way, she swore it.

And Ryan could take a flying leap off the nearest cliff.

She paused for a moment. From what she'd read about him, he might very well do just that, she reflected with apprehension. Him and his bungee-jumping!

With renewed vigor, she pulled the clay toward her and kneaded it like bread dough, bearing down with all her fury until it lay smooth, bubble-free and undeniably defeated.

As she picked up a rolling pin to finish it off, the door swung open and her petite, vivacious assistant breezed in, her pretty brown eyes wide beneath pink, wing-shaped glasses. "You'll never guess who's here. Never, in a million years. Could have knocked me over with a feather, hon."

Fran's voice, quick-paced, gossipy and resonant as a foghorn, held an excitement that could only mean one thing.

"He must be good-looking," guessed Sunny.

"A major hunk." Fran stooped to peer at her reflection in the chrome toaster, combing her dark, pixie-cut hair with long pink fingernails. "Here, in this very hotel," she added for dramatic effect. The only thing Fran liked better than handsome men was high drama.

Sunny was afraid she could guess who the "hunk" might be. She had been somewhat surprised when Ryan had let her have the last word this morning. "Go ahead. Spill it, Fran."

"Your ex," she announced with relish. "In the flesh. And that's some flesh, hon. Hope you don't mind me saying it, but he's six foot three if he's an inch, and when he looked at me with those sexy gray eyes, I thought about ditching Leo and the kids—"

"Where is he?" Sunny interrupted. Her assistant's cheerful gushing had begun to annoy her, although it was nothing out of the ordinary. Sunny suspected any attractive male would be shocked to know the thoughts behind Fran's friendly facade and the appraisals she gave the minute he'd moved out of earshot.

"He's in the lobby." She lifted her lightly penciled brows twice. "Waiting for you."

Sunny's grip on the handles of the rolling pin tightened. "Tell him I'm not in."

Fran stared at her in blatant surprise. "Too late. I already said you are." Her eyes positively sparkled with curiosity. "What gives? I thought you two were friends. I'd be thrilled to death to see him if he was *my* friend."

"I'm ecstatic. Now, please—"

"I sense a story here."

"Just tell him I'm otherwise engaged." Giving in to the curiosity buzzing in her chest, Sunny added, "If he wants to see me, he'll have to make an appointment."

After an incredulous silence, Fran shrugged. "Okay. But you're wasting the perfect opportunity for a high-voltage hug. And if you ask me, it's about time you had a few of those."

"I didn't ask you, Fran."

"Right." With a last glance at her reflection in the toaster, a fluff of her wispy bangs and a tug at the flowered tunic that topped a pink skirt, Fran headed for the lobby.

"Oh, and Fran." Sunny paused, hesitating. "Let me know what he says."

"Every syllable," she vowed.

After what Sunny considered an inordinate length of time, Fran reappeared, her smile expectant and her dark eyes shining. "He made an appointment to see you. Two-thirty."

Sunny glanced at the clock. It was 2:29. She shook her head vehemently. "No. Impossible. I—"

"And he told me to give you this." Fran held up a foil-wrapped bundle. Sunny stared at the package in surprise. What could it possibly be?

"Hey, I don't think it's a rattlesnake or any other deadly creature, hon." Fran shoved the package at her. "Here, open it."

Sunny set it on the clean half of her kitchen table, washed and dried her hands, then loosened the foil.

There, in all its fragrant glory, sat half of a lemon. A *used* half of lemon. Obviously squeezed. Or maybe sucked.

Sunny hid her mouth behind her hand. She wouldn't smile, damn it. She glanced at Fran, who stood gawking at the lemon.

"He gave you a lemon," she observed. "A dried-out lemon." She assessed it silently for a moment. "Nice," she allowed with a nod, always one to give a handsome guy credit. "Not the usual ho-hum type of gift."

Sunny felt her smile growing and bit her bottom lip to stop it. Don't be a pushover, she told herself. Sure, he gives you a sucked lemon today, but, uh, what about tomorrow?

She swallowed a hysterical giggle. Be tough, she told herself. He insulted you. Maligned your character. And yet, a tiny spring of hope bubbled in her heart. Maybe he did still like her a little.

Disgusted with herself, she muttered, "You sucker." Grabbing the lemon, she crushed it violently in her fist, allowing a spurt of juice to trickle down her wrist. "You candy-coated, pansy-brained cream puff." Then she hurled the lemon into the trash.

Looking more than a little stunned, Fran lifted her hands and shrugged. "Okay, okay. So maybe roses would have been better."

Taking a deep breath to calm herself, Sunny washed the lemon juice from her hands at the stainless steel sink. She couldn't remember a time when she had given in to such a multitude of violent impulses.

A masculine voice at the door spun both women around. "Your two-thirty appointment's here," Ryan announced as he strolled into her apartment, cool and self-assured as always.

Sunny stiffened, her heart accelerated, and she resolutely turned her back to him as she dried her hands on her bibbed, blue-checked apron. "Fran, would you tell my two-thirty appointment that I'll have to cancel for today? I'm otherwise engaged."

Before Fran could utter a word, Ryan replied, "Tell her that I'll wait right here until she disengages herself."

"Tell him he may wait in the lobby, or in the parking lot, or in hell until it freezes over."

"Tell her hell froze over a couple of hours ago. I think it's beginning to thaw." In a softer, gentler tone, he added, "And tell her I'm sorry. I was wrong."

Sunny picked up the rolling pin again, intent on blocking out every word he said. Despite her valiant effort, her throat tightened with an alarming threat of tears. *Of all the dirty tricks. The direct approach.*

"Tell him...tell him..." She heard a chair being pulled out from the table, and imagined him settling down to watch her. "Tell him to clear out of my apartment. It's off-limits to the public."

Fran's voice sounded from the doorway. "I think I'll leave you two alone to, uh, battle over old times."

The door swung closed, and silence descended between them. Sunny ignored Ryan with pointed intensity. She busied herself with covering the unused portions of clay in polyethylene sheeting.

With his elbow propped on the table and his chin cupped in his hand, Ryan watched her carry the covered clay across the kitchen. Her honey blond hair was caught up in a knot at the top of her head, with a few ringlets dancing beside her flushed cheek and trailing down the nape of her neck. Her yellow T-shirt and faded jeans were now protected by a bibbed, blue-checked apron that tied in the back, its wide bow emphasizing the narrowness of her waist. And the sleek, feminine curve of her hips.

He forced his attention away from dangerous territory. "Sunny," he said softly, "I truly am sorry. I shouldn't have jumped to conclusions." Why, he wondered, did his emotions always override his common sense where she was concerned? "I was wrong."

She rinsed the clay-matted sponge at the sink, squeezed it out, then returned to her workplace at the kitchen table, where she began rolling a thin sheet of clay into a long, narrow curl. She gave no sign of having heard him.

"I know you didn't take money from my father. I never thought you had until I read your note yesterday."

Her expression didn't actually change, but he noted a hint of a frown in her expressive eyes. She continued rolling her clay— God only knew what for.

"Was your desk clerk right?" he asked, hoping to provoke some verbal response. "Would roses have been better?"

Her full, shapely lips curled up into a scornful smirk at one end. But she said nothing.

"Daisies?" His voice roughened; he forgot to soften it. "Dandelions and Queen Anne's lace?"

At that, very slowly, Sunny raised her gaze to his. Her eyes had never looked greener. A memory flared between them: the wildflower bouquet he'd gathered for her after their first spat. His way of apologizing for his anger when she had refused to make love to him. Long before they had married.

Disgruntled—he hadn't meant to stir up memories—Ryan sat back in the kitchen chair, crossed his arms and muttered, "Flowers didn't work back then, either."

When he again glanced up at her, the dimple was playing in her left cheek. That damned, intriguing dimple. He remembered kissing her there. Softly, oh, so softly, on his way to her mouth.

Quietly, she inquired, "How could my little note make you think that I'd accepted a payoff from your father?"

"My acquisitions director heard a rumor that the other bidder's last name was also Alexander. At first, I thought it might be my father, trying to buy back the mansion. Maybe for his new wife. Or maybe just to foil my plans." Ryan carefully kept the bitterness from his voice. "But then I read your note. It said you wanted to move back there. That you wanted to make a deal. I assumed you were asking me to drop my bid."

"You thought *I* was the other Alexander?" she asked, incredulous. "But..." She hesitated, then continued awkwardly, "I know I've never mentioned this to you—after all, we haven't talked for years, and I knew it wasn't important, although from your Christmas cards I realized you were, uh, under a false impression, but—" She paused again. "My last name's not Alexander."

Her revelation hit him like a swift jab to the stomach. "You took back your maiden name?"

"Yes." Her cheeks were flushed with some emotion he couldn't quite identify.

Tamping down on his own emotional reaction, he shrugged. It meant nothing to him, which name she used. Nothing. "So I'll change it on my mailing list."

She nodded.

He glanced away from her, toward the small, sunny, ruffle-curtained window above the sink. *She hadn't wanted his name.*

"It felt . . . fraudulent," she explained haltingly. "I had no right to the Alexander name." From his peripheral view, he saw that she, too, had focused on some distant point. After a moment, she revived their conversation. "So, I suppose the other bidder *is* your father?"

"Possibly. He was a fool to sell Windsong Place and he's shrewd enough to know it." In a heated undertone, he uttered, "There's no place like it on earth."

At the latent passion in Ryan's usually guarded voice, Sunny overcame her reluctance to look too deeply into his eyes. What she saw there reassured her; lightened her heart. So he *did* still care about something.

As if he realized he had given too much of himself away, Ryan continued with bland nonchalance, "I have someone checking on the other bidder's identity. By the time I get back to my office, I'll know for sure who I'm up against."

Sunny sat down in the chair across from him. "Obviously you never reconciled with your father?"

"Did you really think I had sold out to him?"

Dismay filled her. All this time, she had comforted herself with the notion that she hadn't caused him irreparable harm; that Ryan and his father had made up their differences; that his fortune hadn't been lost and his life hadn't been ruined by their needless marriage.

Her mind flashed back to those emotionally tumultuous days after his father had disowned him. They'd been cast out of Windsong Place—their "Garden of Eden"—and left to scrape together what little money they could to rent an apartment in Asheville. She had been ill with her pregnancy, and Ryan had had to withdraw from his expensive, private university to work full-time at a low-paying job and attend a community college at night. He became obsessed with making his fortune, with proving his worth to a father who refused even to see him. Ryan's happiness had seemed to wither away before her eyes.

But he hadn't complained about any of it. He had sworn to stand by her and their unborn baby, come what may. At twenty years old, he'd been her knight in shining armor. But Sunny had known that inside his armor, he'd been spiritually dying.

"My father visited me after you left, Sunny. He bragged that he had been right about you. Insinuated that you had taken his bribe." Ryan leaned forward, his eyes holding hers with magnetic intensity. "Then he offered to send me back to school. And to reinstate my inheritance." Pushing his chair back from the table, Ryan rose and paced, unable to remain immobile. "Windsong Place had already been sold."

"All these years," Sunny murmured, "I thought . . ."

"What? That I'd sold out? Traded my freedom, my pride, for his money? You should have known me better. I don't need anybody that much. I told him to keep his money. I'd make my own."

"And you did, didn't you. You made your own fortune."

The pure, simple admiration in her eyes caught Ryan off guard. It filled him with a heady rush of exhilaration. As if he had climbed the highest mountain.

"I'm sorry I doubted you," she whispered.

Ryan fought a sudden urge to touch her. "I did what I had to," he replied, oddly embarrassed. "And now I'll do whatever it takes to get my family home back." Disparagingly, he muttered, "Even if they have turned it into a bed-and-breakfast inn."

"Could be worse," Sunny pointed out with an irrepressible sparkle in her eyes that he had almost—*almost*—forgotten about. "I mean, what if they had turned it into a fertilizer factory? Or a nuclear energy plant? Or a toxic waste dump?"

A reluctant half smile tugged at his mouth. "I suppose that might detract a little more from its ambience." After a moment, he explained somberly, "They're selling it as a franchise. Even though I'd own the franchise, Windsong Place would have to remain in operation as it is now, 'A Tanner Bed-'n'-Breakfast Inn,' and the corporate owners would make a percentage of the profit. For the first fifteen years, that is. Then I'd have the option to purchase the property outright, at a preset price."

"So for the next fifteen years, you'd have to open the mansion to the public as an inn, and run it by someone else's rules?"

His eyes narrowed. "You don't think I can do that?"

"You never were very big on rules."

He didn't bother denying that. "I'd hire a manager to follow their rules. That shouldn't be a problem. I would've had to hire a caretaker to keep the place up, even if it were my private residence. Business keeps me on the road." He shrugged. "So I suppose it won't make much difference that guests will be paying to stay there. As long as I can keep a decent manager."

Sunny smiled brightly. "That's where I come in. I'll manage the place for you."

Reclaiming his seat at her table, he propped his chin up on his fist and watched her beneath hooded eyes. "I seem to remember something about you refusing to work for me even if I . . . now, how did you put it? . . . if I pleaded on bended knees?"

"Hey, you sucked a lemon, didn't you?" She waved her slender hand in airy dismissal. "I'll accept that in lieu of your abject begging. *If* you'll verify in writing that the half lemon you gave me was, in fact, personally sucked by you."

"Request denied." And without a conscious thought, he tugged on the shiny golden tendril that curled in front of her delicate ear. The silky texture slid through his fingers and flooded him with memories. Memories of times that he had woven his fingers through her thick, lustrous hair and kissed her until they'd both been damned near delirious.

"Okay, then," she said, obviously unaware of the bothersome thoughts searing through him, "Let's skip the lemon verification documentation." She leaned forward with her elbows on the table. "Let's talk salary. And benefits. And bonuses."

Ryan breathed in deeply. Exhaled slowly. Turned his thoughts to business. In a voice a little too husky, he asked, "Why do you want the job, Sunny?"

Beneath his keen observance, Sunny felt as if a warm, powerful spotlight had been fixed on her, and the entire universe awaited her response. It had always been this way when he bent his entire, concentrated attention upon her. She lifted her chin against sudden nervousness, very similar to stage fright. "I'm at a crossroads in my career. I need more compensation. Financially, I mean. And I have been offered a promotion. But the job would entail traveling across the southeastern states on a regular basis. And, well, you know my grandmother's recovering from heart surgery. I'm not sure how much longer she'll be able to get around on her own. I want to live near her, but she'd rather die than move away from Heaven's Hollow. You know how stubborn she can be."

Ryan's expression turned to one of contemplation.

Encouraged, Sunny reminded him, "She was born and raised in that village. She worked at Windsong Place—for your family— since she was sixteen. She raised your mother there, and you, too. It nearly broke her heart when your father sold the place."

Ryan remembered. Olive, Sunny's grandmother, had been as distraught as Sunny and he, even though she had already retired to a little cottage of her own in nearby Heaven's Hollow.

She had been the closest he'd ever had to a mother.

"I have to find a job near Olive," Sunny concluded, "and you need an innkeeper. What could be more perfect?"

Ryan pondered the idea. He realized he couldn't turn his back on Olive. She had taken care of him for all those years. It was time for him to take care of her. Who was better suited for that job than Sunny?

On the other hand, Sunny would again be in his life, if only on an occasional basis. But she was trouble—always had been, always would be. "Does Olive know that you're, er, applying for this job?"

"No. I didn't want to get her hopes up in case it didn't work out."

"Good. Don't mention it to her."

"Are you . . . turning me down?"

He answered her with a question. "You realize that if I hired you, Sunny, you would be my employee?"

"Yes, of course."

"My computer technology business will keep me mostly in New York, sometimes London, Japan and Korea. But I do intend to spend some time there, at Windsong Place. I'll have a private suite permanently reserved for me."

A little frisson of tension coursed through Sunny. He was, in effect, asking if his presence would cause her a problem. Or if she intended to cause him any problems. She wanted to deny the possibility of either, but doubts assailed her.

Even now, his presence shattered her usual composure. He was like a magnet, drawing her attention away from everything else but him. If the building caught fire around them this very moment, she was afraid she might not even notice.

Determined to hide her doubts, she hedged, "Of course you'll stay there occasionally. It's your home."

Reluctance darkened his eyes. "And you're my ex-wife."

She bristled at the term. "We were friends our entire lives, Ryan. And we were married only three short months." *But those months changed my very soul.* The thought sapped the indignation out of her, replaced it with the same wariness she saw in his face. "We are... friends... aren't we?" she whispered.

His warm, intense stare touched her then. Her hair. Her face. Her mouth. "Yes," he whispered. "Friends."

A tidal wave of warmth swept through her. And an old, familiar longing.

Abruptly Ryan rose and started toward the door, avoiding her eyes. "I'd better be going. And I'm sorry, Sunny. But I—"

He halted midsentence and picked up a framed photograph from the end table in her living room. It was a picture of her grandmother and her, taken many years ago, when they still lived at Windsong Place. Sunny knew that

Ryan recognized the photo. It had been enlarged from a snapshot. But in the original, Ryan had been on Olive's other side.

Sunny had cut him out of the picture.

Ryan's lips tightened almost imperceptibly. He set the framed photograph gently back into its place on the end table. When he lifted his eyes to hers, they looked stark. Empty.

His voice, however, was brisk. "I'll be having the present owners of Windsong Place over for dinner tomorrow night. Wilbur and Lavinia Tanner. Final approval of the sale rests with them. But I don't see too much of a problem. Whatever my rival bids, I'll bid higher. Money usually settles these things."

With one final glance at her—a glance that drew the warmth again to her cheeks—he murmured, "I'll have my secretary arrange a flight for you to New York, and a hotel room for tomorrow night. A car will pick you up around five. You can supervise the catering. If you still want the job."

THE NEXT AFTERNOON, a normal, hectic Friday in Ryan's office, Sunny's phone call interrupted his staff meeting. "What are we serving the Tanners for dinner tonight?"

He drank in her soft, familiar voice like a soothing cup of honeyed tea. He sorely needed soothing at the moment. He had just learned for a fact the identity of the rival bidder. Edgar Rockwell Alexander. His father. It seemed he wanted Windsong Place as a wedding present for his new bride.

Ironic.

"Ryan?" prompted Sunny. "Are you there?"

"Yes. And we'll be serving lobster Newburg. Tanner's secretary told mine it's his favorite dish." He conjured up a vision of Sunny's face; imagined her alone in a hotel room. And suddenly she no longer soothed him. In fact, his turmoil worsened. *I'll have to see her tonight.* Why the hell had he hired her? *For Olive's sake.*

"Who's catering dinner?" she asked.

"Hampton Bay Restaurant."

"I don't think that's a good idea."

Ryan pulled the receiver away from his ear and stared at it, as if he could send her his frown through the wires. She hadn't even started the job yet and already she was questioning his decisions. That was a problem he hadn't anticipated, though he should have, of course. From the time she was six, she'd refused to take orders. He'd have to remind her who was boss.

"Sunny, do you have any idea how many employees I have?"

"What does that have to do with tonight's dinner?"

"Last time I checked, the count was well over two thousand. What do you think would happen if every one of those employees questioned every decision I made?"

"I hate to clue you in, Ry, but they probably do." She said it in such a light, joking manner that he couldn't take offense, even if he'd tried. He could clearly hear her smile. And envision it. Damn her. She went on merrily. "Anyway, congratulations on your employee count. I'm honored to be among the thousands. Now, let's get back to tonight. Wilbur Tanner doesn't trust restaurant cooking, unless it's from his own restaurant. Something about food poisoning when he was younger."

Ryan cradled his forehead in his palm. After tonight, he wouldn't deal personally with Sunny. He'd have one of his middle managers check on her progress. Someone with nerves of steel. "How could you possibly know what Wilbur Tanner likes?"

"His chef told me."

"You talked to his chef?"

"Sure. We *have* to know what the Tanners like and don't like. How else could we be sure they'd enjoy the dinner? If we can't make one evening pleasurable for them, how could they expect us to make the inn's guests happy? Anyway, the chef swore that Wilbur Tanner would know if food had been commercially prepared the moment he put it in his mouth."

"Sunny, that's ridiculous."

"Maybe so, but I feel very strongly that we should serve a nice, home-cooked meal."

Ryan closed his eyes and shook his head. When Sunny "felt very strongly" about anything, chances were she had a plan of action waiting in the wings. He sincerely hoped not. "Now you sound like your grandmother. A nice home-cooked meal is Olive's answer to world peace. But I'm not going to cancel my restaurant order." His tone, though quiet, brooked no opposition. "The Tanners will love Hampton Bay's lobster Newburg. Trust me, Sunny. Everything will be fine."

Looking back, Ryan would come to realize those last words had been as naive as Custer's charge on Little Bighorn.

3

AT FIVE O'CLOCK Friday afternoon, a limousine delivered Sunny from an elegant New York hotel to the exclusive Manhattan address where Ryan lived.

Alone in the spacious apartment, where the satiny walls, plush carpet and contemporary furniture were all a stark white and accessorized by violet and chrome, Sunny felt like a trespasser.

This was Ryan's private domain; the place he now called home. But as she ventured out of the tiled foyer to inspect the living room, she saw no trace of the man she had once known.

Even his bedroom, which she couldn't resist peeking into, was devoid of his personality. Where were his bookshelves crammed with military novels, sports almanacs and westerns? Where were the photos of his dogs and horses? Or the novelty items he had brought home for her to marvel over whenever he traveled?

Someone else, she decided, had decorated the place. A question throbbed in her chest. Who? On her way past the sofa, she wondered who cuddled up with him there. The cozy table in the breakfast nook made her wonder who shared his morning muffins. And as she gazed at his king-size bed with its multicolored, jewel-toned designer spread, the questions grew too acute to contemplate. She hurried past the bed without subjecting herself to a second glance.

In the bathroom, his masculine toiletries and the lingering scent of his after-shave brought with them a nostalgic pang, a haunting sense of loss. No, she definitely shouldn't be here.

However, she had an important job to do. She would hostess his dinner party and help win the Tanners' approval. She had, after all, been a key factor in his loss of Windsong Place. It was only fitting that she help him win it back.

Besides, Olive needed her to live nearby, and to earn enough money to help pay medical bills. High-paying jobs weren't exactly plentiful in the rural mountain community of Heaven's Hollow. A job at Windsong Place seemed the only answer. The sale *had* to go through.

With determination shielding her from the worst of her imaginings about Ryan and his current life-style, Sunny headed toward the huge, gleaming kitchen to start work.

Two hours flew by and before she realized it the Tanners were due to arrive. With relief, she heard Ryan call from the foyer, "I'm home."

The greeting, a common one heard in almost any household, struck Sunny with another pang of nostalgia. Here she was, setting his dinner table, chilling his wine, preparing for his evening meal. And there he was, calling, "I'm home."

Why should that bother her so?

This was business, she reminded herself. Purely business. And when his guests left, so would she.

She caught only a glimpse of him on his way to the bedroom. After a quick shower and shave, he emerged in a cashmere jacket and black pleated trousers. His suntanned skin glowed with dark beauty against the white silk of his shirt. His raven hair glinted; his after-shave exuded an elegant, woodsy scent.

With a fluttering in her stomach, Sunny swore he grew more handsome by the hour. And more distant, if that were possible.

He had barely acknowledged her presence before the doorman buzzed the intercom, announcing the arrival of their guests. *His* guests, Sunny corrected herself. She was only the hired help.

"One thing, Sunny." He cast her a quick cool glance as he sauntered past her toward the foyer. "Don't mention my family's connection to Windsong Place. I'd prefer they don't know until after the negotiations. Any perceived sentimental value will strengthen their sense of bargaining power."

Sunny nodded, trying to ignore her disappointment at his curt, businesslike air. It seemed as if he were deliberately reminding her of their employer-employee relationship.

"Also," he continued, "I'd prefer not to disclose my blood-tie with the other bidder. Unless the Tanners bring it up."

"Fine." Sunny adopted the same brusque, impersonal manner. "Since we're on the subject, there's another aspect of our situation that I must insist we keep to ourselves."

Ryan raised his brows arrogantly. As if surprised that a mere underling would address him with such familiarity.

Sunny's tone emerged a bit colder than it otherwise might have. "I'd rather not mention our past relationship. It might be awkward for everyone if my future business associates think of me as your . . . ex-wife." Her voice had lost some of its haughtiness on the last word. How she hated the term! It branded her as a problem in his life, and not even a recent one, at that. Yesterday's bad news, already discarded. She didn't want to be considered his "ex" anything.

His gaze grew even cooler. "Of course I won't mention our past relationship. I wouldn't want to embarrass you, Sunny."

Her name, uttered in his soft, virile, southern voice, activated the fluttering inside her again. Except it felt higher this time. Somewhere around her heart.

WILBUR TANNER'S SMILE flashed in his florid face beneath a thick white mustache as he talked baseball. He spoke with the bluntness of a midwesterner and gestured with a lit cigar.

Lavinia Tanner, with her dark hair lacquered into an immobile coiffure, her aristocratic nose held high and her slender back erect, sat in bored silence beside her short, white-haired husband on the sofa.

Sunny recognized the warning signs; the woman disapproved of something. She suspected it had to do with her. But what?

Not her appearance, surely. She had chosen a classic herringbone-tweed jacket with a straight, calf-length black skirt and cowl-necked sweater. Why would anyone object to that? But surprisingly enough, Ryan hadn't seemed approving, either.

A mortifying thought hit her. Maybe she didn't measure up to his usual female company. Names of beauties who had been connected with him in society pages and gossip columns came back to taunt her. Wealthy women with a sophistication born of money. While she, when all was said and done, was merely the granddaughter of his domestic help.

And his "ex."

She raised her chin; squared her shoulders. She didn't have to measure up to anybody. She was here in a professional capacity, and she would prove her worth, businesswise, by the results of her efforts.

Determined to draw Lavinia into conversation, Sunny talked about her experience managing hotels, and even forced Lavinia to murmur an answer or two concerning Windsong Place.

Wilbur, meanwhile, trotted off to make a phone call. Ryan took advantage of his absence to inspect his newest employee. How different she looked than she ever had before. The difference surprised him. And annoyed the pure, living hell out of him.

Her tailored suit, a far cry from her blue jeans, conveyed cool professionalism. A chic style for a female executive. Apparel that shouted "Purely business. Keep your hands off."

Had she worn it with him in mind? Was she trying to send *him* that message? Ryan's gaze traveled over her austere outfit. If so, she'd taken unnecessary precautions. He hadn't the slightest interest in her personally. And if he had, it would take a whole lot more than clothing to stop him. He remembered what lay beneath those clothes—in intimate detail. And how to make her cool green eyes grow sultry...

His body responded to the mental images, and with a silent curse he turned his attention elsewhere...to her hair. Thick, lush curls, all shiny and soft, and smelling of lilies. Taking a mouthful of wine, Ryan felt his vexation growing. What kind of protection would a business suit give her against some randy bastard if her hair looked like that? The first thing a man wanted to do was thrust his fingers into its softness. Inhale its fragrance. Spread its golden beauty across his bed pillows ...

Ryan's hand tightened involuntarily around his wineglass. At a sudden, inaudible *snap* and a slight pain in his right palm, he realized the delicate crystal stem of the glass had cracked.

Fortunately, no one seemed to notice. Keeping his hand closed to conceal the broken stem, Ryan excused himself and headed for the kitchen.

Sunny, meanwhile, had run fresh out of one-sided chatter. Silence had fallen again between Lavinia and her. As she considered refilling the appetizer tray with vegetables, cheese and crackers, Lavinia startled her by initiating conversation.

"So tell me, Sunny, do you have children?"

The question rendered Sunny speechless. *Children*. Of all the subjects Lavinia could have broached, why did it have to be this one? "No," she finally managed to reply. "No children."

Wistfulness, though mellowed by time, burned a hurtful path through her. She *should* have had a child. He would have been ten by now. Maybe with Ryan's thickly lashed eyes, or his wavy black hair, or that devilish, crooked grin of his. A thickness formed in Sunny's throat. She cut her gaze away from Lavinia.

And met Ryan's.

He had obviously overheard the question on his way back from the kitchen. And though Wilbur had returned to his seat, too, and had begun talking about the recent winner of the Kentucky Derby, Ryan's attention was directed solely to Sunny.

The knot in her throat swelled bigger. She thought she had overcome this sensitivity. Many times in the past ten years she had talked about children, played with them, held newborn infants, even daydreamed about having one of her own. So why should she choke up now?

Ryan then did a very unexpected thing. He winked at her. A special wink, full of purpose, executed without a smile. *Something's up. Something new and interesting.*

A tingling anticipation washed through Sunny. A reflex, surely, from years gone by. And though she knew the anticipation to be groundless, its warmth gradually dissolved the tight ache in her throat.

Ryan held her gaze for an appraising moment, then turned his attention to Wilbur's conversation. Sunny struggled with a rush of affection for him. He cared! She hugged the revelation close to her. Another part of her—the realistic part—contradicted, He just hadn't wanted his hostess to ruin the dinner party with hysterics over their lost baby.

Lavinia brought Sunny out of her reverie with a quiet remark. "How romantic," she said, having caught Ryan and Sunny's gaze.

"Romantic?" Sunny's eyes snapped back to Lavinia's watchful ones. "Ryan and I? Oh, no, you're mistaken. Very mistaken. Our relationship is anything but romantic."

Acutely embarrassed—and very glad Ryan hadn't overheard *that* part of their conversation—Sunny announced that dinner was almost ready and retreated to the kitchen.

Lavinia's remark had jolted her. How could she have jumped to such a false conclusion? As Sunny filled the silver serving dishes, she realized her hands were trembling.

Wilbur led the rest of the party into the dining room with a cigar clamped between his teeth. He smiled at Sunny as she lit the candles on the dining room table. Patting his stomach, he rumbled, "I'm starved, Sunny. What's on the menu tonight?"

Ryan answered from behind him, "Lobster Newburg."

Wilbur removed the cigar from his mouth and raised his white, bushy brows. "Doesn't smell like lobster Newburg."

With a mild sense of surprise, Ryan realized he was right. It didn't smell the least like lobster Newburg. He'd been so distracted, he hadn't noticed.

"There's been a change in the menu," Sunny informed them. "No lobster Newburg tonight." Three pairs of questioning eyes awaited an explanation. "Don't you just love surprises?" She smiled and gestured for everyone to be seated.

Ryan explained with urbane smoothness, "Sunny is famous for her, uh, surprises." As he pulled out a chair for her, he whispered against her fragrant golden hair, "You canceled the restaurant order?"

She nodded, avoiding his eyes.

"What did you make?"

"The most gourmet thing I know how to cook."

Her answer did not reassure him. Ryan seated himself beside her and admirably maintained his smile. What the hell else could he do? He tried to forget the last time he'd seen her cook. She had melted the frying pan. Mentally he braced himself for whatever might come. He'd take up the matter of her insubordination with her later. *If* they survived the meal.

The elegance of the table mollified him somewhat. Crisp linen napkins, silver serving dishes, long-stemmed roses and candles in crystal holders enhanced the aura of fine dining.

Sunny lifted the lid off the largest serving tray with an impressive flourish. Ryan stared at the main course. Wilbur and Lavinia stared at the main course. In silence.

"Tacos," Sunny explained.

"Tacos?" repeated Wilbur, frowning.

"Tacos," noted Ryan in a strangled tone.

"How lovely!" Lavinia's delighted cry surprised everybody. "I adore tacos. We had them in a little seaside café in Mexico. It was on our honeymoon. *Before* Wilbur stopped eating at restaurants." She eagerly lifted one onto her plate.

"Are these homemade?" Wilbur studied his plate suspiciously. "Can't eat restaurant food. Never agrees with me. Meant to warn you ahead of time, but it slipped my mind."

"Yes, certainly they're homemade," Sunny assured him. "Right down to the corn tortillas."

"I'll know if they're not. I can tell the minute I put 'em in my mouth."

"They're homemade, I swear."

With a dubious expression, Wilbur took his first bite. Swallowed. Took another. "Homemade," he confirmed.

"Delicious," pronounced Lavinia between crunches. "Every dinner we attend, it seems they serve lobster Newburg. How refreshing to have something *I* like instead of Wilbur's old standby. He's probably tired of lobster Newburg, too. Whatever gave you the idea to serve tacos, Sunny?"

"Research," she replied, trying to turn the success to its fullest advantage. "Ryan always says it's important to ask the right questions and, above all, be prepared. It's the only way to please the customer. Or, the guests, as the case may be."

Lavinia smiled her approval, and Sunny chanced a peek at Ryan. He was staring at her in something akin to wonderment.

"Wilbur, darling," cooed Lavinia, "*you* must have told Sunny how much I like tacos." For the first time that evening, she beamed a loving smile at her husband. "And here

I thought you'd forgotten my fondness for them. Aren't you the sly one, acting surprised."

Perplexed but smiling, Wilbur shrugged and helped himself to another taco, refried beans, guacamole salad and rice.

Lavinia's animation dispersed all traces of tension. The conversation flowed from favorite restaurants, Lavinia's contribution, to worst restaurants, Wilbur's, each anecdote elevating the mood.

While Sunny talked, Ryan watched her gesture expressively and punctuate her story with peals of laughter. *This* was how he remembered her. Bright-eyed, spontaneous and bubbling with contagious gaiety. Impossible to look at her like this without seeing his eighteen-year-old bride.

Disturbed beyond all reason, Ryan pushed his plate away barely touched. And found Lavinia watching him.

Soon, he assured himself, this would all be over. Sunny would be gone again. Middle management could deal with her. And he would head out for the mountains. Find new ledges to climb. Ride the highest ridges. Store up enough thrills to stave off the inevitable emptiness.

"LAVINIA'S BEEN CRANKY lately," confided Wilbur as he lit an after-dinner cigar. He and Ryan had settled into armchairs in the living room with snifters of brandy. "She complains that I don't think about her anymore. I'm going to let her think I suggested those tacos, if that's okay with you."

Ryan nodded, hiding his surprise at Wilbur's personal confidence. He himself would never air private problems of that nature—if he *had* private problems of that nature—to anyone, let alone a stranger. In fact, he suddenly realized, the only person he had ever confided in, to any degree, was Sunny.

A lifetime ago.

As the men turned their discussion to finance, Lavinia insisted on helping Sunny carry dishes to the sink. When they were alone in the kitchen, she awarded Sunny a grateful smile. "Those tacos brought back fond memories of my honeymoon in Mexico." She sighed in contentment and, with a sideways glance, queried, "Where did you and Ryan spend yours?"

Relaxed from her dinner success and mellowed by laughter, Sunny replied, "We didn't travel very far. We ended up just staying at Windsong Place." With a smile, she reminisced, "Oh, but it was *heaven*, though...."

It took only a moment longer for Sunny to realize what she had said. Embarrassment shot through her. And self-recrimination. If only she could take back the words!

Lavinia's bottom jaw had lowered. "You spent your honeymoon at Windsong Place?"

Mortified, Sunny realized that not only had she spilled the beans about their past relationship, but she had also opened the door for way too many questions. Questions Ryan hadn't wanted asked, let alone answered.

Lavinia clasped her hands together in delight. "Oh, Sunny, how perfect! How absolutely perfect. I sensed that you regarded the place as more than just a cold business deal. You honeymooned there! It must have been while we were at another location. We have fifteen of them to oversee, you know. Oh, wait until I tell Wilbur. What suite did you stay in?"

"It was a long time ago," Sunny hedged weakly.

"Do you remember the color of the wallpaper? We've tried to keep all the same color schemes in the bedrooms."

"Blue. With pink Victorian cabbage roses in the trim."

"I know exactly which one you mean. In the southeast corner of the inn. French doors lead to a balcony, right? One of my favorite suites. Oh, Sunny, I must say, you've changed my mind about Ryan." Lavinia squeezed her arm in an affectionate, motherly way.

"I have?"

"Certainly. I thought he wanted the inn strictly for the investment value. You know how these self-made tycoons can be . . . all dollars and cents, with no appreciation of the finer things. I even thought Ryan might be considering absentee ownership. Which I deplore. I misunderstood the situation entirely. To be honest, I didn't even realize he was married. When Wilbur sidestepped my question about his marital status, I was certain he was single."

"Well, actually—"

"When we arrived this evening, the first thing I noticed was your lack of a wedding ring. And then when Ryan introduced you as Sunny Shannon, his 'general manager,' as he put it, I was sure you two weren't married. I was ready to leave right then and there, and to sell the inn to our other bidder. But then, the way you gazed at each other across the room—" Lavinia all but sighed.

Sunny felt herself blanch. *Had* she gazed at Ryan in some doltish way?

"Is Shannon your maiden name, or your middle?"

"My maiden name. But—"

"Oh, you modern women, keeping your maiden names instead of taking your husbands'. In my time, no one even thought of it. Anyway, Sunny, I'm so pleased Ryan is happily married. The first thing I look for in a franchisee is a solid marriage."

"You do?" replied Sunny, astounded.

"Absolutely. I would never again sell one of our franchises to an unmarried man. We learned our lesson a year ago with our New England location. So irresponsible, that bachelor was, chasing women, throwing wild parties, causing all kinds of scandals with our female guests. Things like that can ruin our corporate image. We're a family resort, Sunny, and we want every one of our inns to keep its mom-and-pop ambience." Leaning closer, she whispered, "There's only one thing worse than a single man, and that's a divorced one. We learned *that* lesson at our Hawaiian location."

Sunny gazed at her in mute agony.

Lavinia confided in a chatty tone, "I try to keep a close eye on all of our resorts, but with fifteen of them, it's difficult. That's why we must franchise them out to people who really *care* about them." With another maternal squeeze of Sunny's arm, Lavinia said, "I'll have to tell Wilbur that I approve of the sale. He can't sell without me, you know. I might not use my maiden name, sister, but I do own half of the corporation." She smiled, obviously well pleased with herself. "Come, dear. I'll tell Wilbur that I approve."

Indecision roiled within Sunny. Should she tell the truth...and lose Windsong Place for Ryan a second time?

Heartsick with apprehension, Sunny trailed Lavinia to the living room. If Ryan denied their "marriage," Lavinia would think she had deliberately misled her. She had to speak to him alone.

Wilbur and Ryan stood near the expansive window that overlooked Manhattan, gazing down at the sea of city lights, discussing the performance of the New York Yankees. Lavinia tapped her husband's shoulder, interrupting his lengthy discourse, and whispered into his ear.

Before Sunny could warn Ryan of their predicament, Wilbur announced, "I've made up my mind, Alexander. The franchise is yours. We'll work out details of the sale at Windsong Place."

Sunny saw the flush of triumph rise beneath Ryan's tan. He turned his eyes to her and she saw gratitude there .

"Drive down next weekend, if you can," invited Wilbur. "And of course, bring your wife."

A perplexed frown drew Ryan's dark eyebrows together. "My wife? But I'm not—"

"Congratulations, honey!" In desperation, Sunny slid her arms around his neck. And tried to silence him with a kiss.

He jerked back from her in surprise. "What in the—"

To stop his mouth from forming words, she planted her lips against his. Firmly. She felt his muscles tense to absolute stillness. His breathing seemed to have stopped.

How ridiculous she'd look, she suddenly realized, if her alleged husband pulled away and scowled! But after a prickly, heart-pounding moment, his arms came up around her. And he responded to her kiss. Thoroughly.

He commandeered her mouth with searing, sensual mastery, his kiss deep and rousing and potent as the finest brandy.

Intoxicating her.

When the kiss ended, only his iron-strong arms kept Sunny upright. She felt dizzy. Overheated. Forgetful of where she was. And shocked by the intensity of her response.

That shock was mirrored in Ryan's silver gray eyes.

Wilbur's throaty chuckle intruded. "Must be newlyweds. Don't know why I thought you were single."

Ryan couldn't seem to find a voice. Neither could Sunny. She disengaged herself from his embrace slowly, as if any sudden movement might tear her racing heart right out of her chest.

"Well, he's not single," interjected Lavinia. "He's a stable, hardworking married man. The only kind we Tanners would trust with our corporate name." To Ryan, she explained, "Tanner Inns are, first and foremost, *family* inns. We intend to keep the mom-and-pop atmosphere at every one of our locations. Experts say it can't be done. I disagree." With a superior smile, she continued, "So we must be very picky about who runs them. And, as I explained to Sunny, a strong marriage speaks well of a person's moral fiber."

Wilbur chimed in with the enthusiasm of a sports announcer, "It was a close decision between you and another bidder. Very close. Down to the wire. Funny—his name's Alexander, too. Edgar Rockwell Alexander. He's not related to you, is he?"

Sunny saw a muscle flex in Ryan's jaw. "Distantly."

Lavinia crowed, "I thought there might be a connection. We bought the house from him originally, you know. He wants it back. Badly. But you two are just the kind of couple I'm looking for to run our inns. Come now, Wilbur, it's time for us to go." On her way to the door, Lavinia murmured to Sunny, "Thank you for dinner, dear. See you at Windsong Place."

"EXPLAIN ONE THING to me, Sunny. Just one damned thing," thundered Ryan. "How the hell did I acquire a wife over dinner?"

Sunny winced. "You're yelling, Ryan."

Scowling at her, he shoved an unruly lock of hair back from his forehead and continued pacing across the living room. He knew full well how the fiasco had happened. He had heard Lavinia's monologue regarding the inn's family atmosphere and the superior moral character of married men. He understood that Sunny had acted with his best interests at heart. He knew he shouldn't be yelling, knew he shouldn't be shaking inside.

But he was. And all because of that damned kiss.

She'd caught him completely off guard. Her mouth against his had ignited a fuse that sizzled up his spine. Never had a kiss exploded inside him like that one had. Before he could think, he had pulled her closer. Kissed her deeper, harder. But not nearly long enough . . .

"I'm sorry, Ryan," apologized Sunny with quiet dignity, "but Lavinia jumped to the conclusion we were married. What was I supposed to do?"

Anything but kiss me, he thought, furious with her and himself.

"Would it have been better to ruin our chances without even discussing the matter with you?"

Yes. Much better. But of course, it wouldn't have been. He wanted Windsong Place now more than he had at the outset. "Our relationship is none of Lavinia's business," he growled. "Or anyone else's. My marital status should have nothing to do with my eligibility as a franchisee. I'm up against blind prejudice here. Discrimination against single men."

"And divorced men," Sunny concurred. "They're even worse."

Ryan's quelling frown chastised her. He then sat down heavily into the armchair. "How did it happen, Sunny? How did Lavinia jump to such a farfetched conclusion?"

Groping for words, Sunny lifted her hands to explain. But no explanation came to mind. Finally she mumbled, "What does it matter? What's done is done, and—"

"Sunny." His stern gaze demanded cooperation. "Talk."

She bit the inside of her cheek. Considered refusing. But slowly, reluctantly, swallowed her pride. "I told her about our honeymoon."

He stared at her, uncomprehending. "Our honeymoon?"

"Yes. Our honeymoon."

"But, Sunny, we didn't have a honeymoon."

"That's basically what I told her. That we...stayed...at Windsong Place. She didn't realize we lived there at the time."

"Thank you for that, Sunny. Thank you for keeping at least one of the secrets we agreed to keep."

Stung, she snapped, "You're blaming this on me, aren't you." When Ryan didn't even bother to deny it, she pursed her lips, glanced away from him, exhaled and decided to address the real problem—his need for an attitude adjustment. Employing a counseling technique learned in the course of her management experience, she said, "You think you're angry at me, but if you breathe deeply and count to ten, you will realize that you're really angry at the Tanners. They're the ones who will only sell to a married man. So why sit here and browbeat me?"

"I'm not browbeating you, whatever the hell that is. But we *had* agreed to keep our past relationship a secret. Somehow I don't think describing our honeymoon to dinner guests is quite conducive to that goal, do you?"

"I didn't *describe* our honeymoon," she protested, embarrassed by the thought. Her cheeks heated with sudden guilt as she remembered saying, *Oh, but it was heaven, though....*

In a voice just a trifle too smooth and bland, Ryan inquired, "Exactly what did you say about it, then?"

Sunny stared at him, aghast. She couldn't tell him. Not when the aftershock of his kiss still quivered in the depths of her stomach, and long-ago memories of his lovemaking echoed through her very soul. "Never mind," she said with a dismissive wave of her hand. "That's beside the point. But I did not purposely tell Lavinia about us."

"Of course not. She probably laced your guacamole with sodium Pentothal."

At last, his chiding had succeeded in angering her. Sunny rose stiffly from the sofa, her fists clenched at her sides. "I've had about all I'm going to take from you." Furiously, she marched to the coat closet.

"Where do you think you're going?"

"Home, that's where." She flung the closet door open and snatched her raincoat from its hanger. "I was crazy to think I could ever work for you. I seriously pity the two thousand other fools who—"

"Sit back down there," Ryan commanded, rising to his feet and pointing at the sofa as if he were a monarch issuing a royal edict. "We're not finished."

"Yes, we are." With her long gray coat draped over her forearm, she walked briskly to the door.

"So you haven't really changed, after all."

With the door partially opened, her hand on the knob, Sunny halted. And turned back to glower into his dark, sullen face. "What do you mean by that?"

"Again, you're leaving when the going gets rough."

Guilt, anger, sorrow, dismay—all knifed through her at once. "What are you referring to?" she whispered. "Our divorce?" The unfairness of his implied accusation shoved its way to the forefront of her chaotic emotions. She had left him during the roughest of times, yes. But by leaving, she had made things better for him. Or so she had thought. His father had promised her he'd reconcile with Ryan and reinstate his inheritance if—and only if—she left him, and kept their bargain a secret. Which she had. "Are you saying I left you because life got tough?"

"I didn't think so at the time." As Ryan ambled toward her, his eyes grew turbulent, like a stormy gray sea. "Now I'm not so sure."

She drew in a quick, pained breath. She couldn't tolerate his doubt. "You know why I left," she said, her voice strident with passion. "You agreed that I should. Because you—we—our baby..." Her throat closed, cutting off her words. If he had wanted her to stay, she would have.

"Yes." His whisper was fierce. "I told you to go. There was no reason for you to stay." His hands swept up and bracketed her jawline, his fingertips buried in her hair. "But now there is."

She stared up into the troubled, silvery eyes that had haunted her dreams, dominated her memories, intruded into her every relationship. Why had she contacted him again? *Get out of here, Sunny,* cried her survival instinct. *Run.*

His ruggedly handsome face loomed dangerously near as he whispered, "I want my home back, Sunny. I want Windsong Place." He leaned his muscled shoulder against the door she had opened, and forced it to a definite close. "And you're going to help me get it."

Half-afraid of the answer she might receive, Sunny pressed her back to the doorjamb for support as she summoned her courage. "How?"

His eyes dallied with hers; his fingers lingered on the curve of her jawline. "You're going to be my wife." And then, like the sun disappearing behind a storm cloud, his intensity suddenly cooled. He dropped his hands from her face. "Or so we'll let them think...until the contract is signed."

4

THE NEXT DAY, after Sunny had returned to Atlanta, Ryan called her with a message from Lavinia. The invitation to spend next weekend at Windsong Place had been extended—the Tanners requested their company for the week.

And Ryan had accepted. For both of them.

"A whole week!" exclaimed Sunny, dismayed at the thought of spending all that time in Ryan's company—*as his wife.* "But I thought you were just going to work out details of the sale."

"Lavinia's come up with some harebrained scheme," Ryan muttered. "She wants you to call her." After a pause, he asked, "You will be able to stay the week, right?" When Sunny hesitated, he added, "You do want the management position?"

"I'll see if I can arrange for personal leave."

"Good. Call Lavinia." Without another word, he hung up.

Sunny scowled at the receiver. If she hadn't wanted the job so badly, she'd have told him to shove it. A few moments later, in the privacy of her apartment, she telephoned Lavinia.

"Sunny, dear, I'm thrilled that you'll be spending next week with us. I have a fabulous idea. Since you'll soon be in charge of organizing the activities at Windsong Place, why not give you a little taste of what lies in store for you?"

"A little taste?"

"Why don't you plan activities for the week? We won't actually involve our guests this time. That would be difficult to arrange on such short notice. This will simply be a trial run. Wilbur and I will act as *your* guests and sample your activities. Doesn't that sound like fun?"

What Lavinia was actually proposing, Sunny realized, was an audition. To see if she could entertain the inn's guests to Lavinia's satisfaction.

She responded with appropriate enthusiasm. What else could she do? The success of the sale might now depend on her. Squaring her chin, she resolved to do her best. She did, after all, have extensive experience in hotel management. It didn't, however, include the organization of social activities beyond a display of brochures in the lobby. But she would do her best.

The first thing she did was call Ryan. She'd need expense money to bring this thing together.

"Spend whatever you need," he instructed. "Let's do this thing right." That was all she needed to hear. Along with his credit card number, of course.

DURING THE WEEK preceding her trip to Windsong Place, Sunny shifted around schedules of her assistant managers, contacted the chamber of commerce closest to Windsong Place for brochures on community attractions, worked out a plan of social activities, designed her agenda into a colorful brochure, shipped materials she would need to carry out the activities, listened to local musicians who could play a few evenings at Windsong Place and quickly refurbished her wardrobe with a whirlwind, last-minute shopping trip.

Incredibly, she was ready by Friday, although somewhat frazzled, dressed in her new white eyelet peasant blouse and a tiered, multiprint skirt.

Before leaving for the airport, Sunny gave last-minute instructions to Fran, along with the number of Ryan's cellular phone, in case she needed to reach her in an emergency.

"Not that it's any of my business, hon," complained Fran in a discreet whisper from behind the front desk, "but last weekend you were at each other's throats. Now you're going away with him for a week?"

Sunny felt her color rise. "It's not what you think, Fran. There's nothing between Ryan and me except business that has to be cleared up. Just hold down the fort while I'm gone, okay?"

"Sure. I'm bucking for a promotion, remember? But—"

"And if my grandmother calls, just tell her I'm away on business. *Don't* say I'm with Ryan. Don't even mention his name." As Fran opened her mouth to ask more questions, Sunny added, "And don't ditch Leo and the kids for any handsome customers. The last thing you need in your life is an 'ex.'"

With those words of wisdom, Sunny turned her back on her friend's lively curiosity and hurried off to catch her flight.

As they had planned, Ryan met her punctually in a sleek black sports car at the Asheville airport—the closest one to the small mountain community near Windsong Place.

If she had expected warmth or gratitude from him for her compliance in this crazy mock-marriage scheme of his, she would have been sadly disappointed. He greeted her with a civil but cool "good afternoon," then spent the first leg of their journey talking business on his cellular phone.

Although she understood barely half of the technical jargon he used, Sunny deduced he was directing his technicians in developing some new computer software. When she thought of how he had revolutionized the computer world with his innovative software, she experienced another rush of pride in him. Knowing that he had accomplished this without money or assistance from his father—whose corporation had formerly set the international pace for computer technology—her pride turned into awe.

All those hours Ryan had spent at his computer during their childhood had obviously paid off. Every evening, when other kids would have been watching television, Ryan had been mulling over his father's old computer manuals and experimenting at his computer screen. From the time he was nine years old, he had entered his own work in science and media contests, winning prize after prize for his creative programming.

She remembered carefully clipping every article from newspapers that had mentioned his awards, collecting them in a scrapbook, and marveling over each ribbon and certificate that had been presented to him.

He'd pushed himself so desperately hard. And though he had never admitted it, Sunny knew he'd done it to please his father. To make him proud. To gain a smidgeon of his attention. Many times she had watched Ryan approach Edgar Rockwell Alexander, world-renowned computer tycoon, on one of his rare visits to Windsong Place. Sunny could clearly visualize the hopeful expectancy on Ryan's then-boyish face—and with an intensity far too serious for his years—as he brought forth the astounding fruits of his labor: a program, an award, a write-up in the paper. . . .

An almost-forgotten ache filled Sunny as she remembered. The hope in Ryan's youthful eyes never had survived these encounters. He'd been turned away without so much as a pat on the head. Edgar Alexander had barely taken the time to glance at the intricate programs his motherless son had designed.

Shocked at how much the thought still hurt, Sunny shook away the pain. The world itself had acknowledged Ryan's brilliance. He no longer needed the approval of his father.

"Do you still design your own software?" she asked curiously, "now that you're head of a corporation?"

Ryan's gaze flickered to her in surprise. "Not usually. I have programmers to do that now. I supervise them."

She raised her brows. "But you always loved designing programs. Don't you miss it?"

He shrugged. "I haven't given it much thought." After a moment, he remarked, "At least I've turned my passion into a living. Why haven't you done the same with your art?"

"I tried. But it isn't easy to pay rent and put food on the table—" *and pay hospital bills* "—when you're an unknown with no capital to see you through the rough times. You've heard the term 'starving artist,' haven't you?"

"A cop-out, if ever I heard one."

She bristled. "Think whatever you'd like. At least I *am* making a living, doing something that I enjoy." On a softer note, she added, "Maybe someday I'll have the chance to devote more time to my art. Maybe sell a few of my pieces."

She fell silent, immersed in a dream she had almost forgotten. A gallery, a showplace. Perhaps a small following of customers to ooh and aah over her work.

Ryan clicked off his recorder as he finished dictating notes, and silence reigned within the sports car.

Sunny studied his strong, handsome profile. He looked much more casual this morning than he had at his dinner party. His dark hair was tousled, with an errant lock falling across his forehead. The sleeves of his midnight-blue sweater were pushed up to his elbows. He wore jeans. Tight, faded jeans that hugged his narrow hips and long, powerful legs.

What am I doing, noticing his hips and legs? Sunny berated herself. *Think of him as your employer.* "Employer" somehow seemed safer than friend. She had tried "friend," and where had it gotten her? Devastated by one power-packed kiss. A kiss that probably hadn't meant a thing to him.

But she wouldn't think about the kiss. She'd never be able to spend the week with him if she thought about the kiss . . . and how it had burned away every ounce of her good sense. She could have gone on kissing him forever. . . .

"Before I forget, look in the glove compartment," he instructed. His soft, deep drawl put an end to her reverie, and she realized she had been staring at him.

Curious, Sunny did as she was told and pulled out a small box. A ring box. "What's this?"

"Your costume." His voice sounded grim. "Try it on."

Nestled in the black velvet box was a wide, diamond-encrusted wedding band. An elegant, expensive ring—much showier than the simple band of gold he had slipped onto her finger ten years ago. Even though she realized he was giving her this ring now for purely strategic purposes, she hesitated to lift it from the box.

A part of her had died the day she'd given him back his wedding band. The idea of wearing one now disconcerted her.

But of course, she understood the necessity. Slowly, she extracted the ring from its velvet bed. Her eyes lighted on his left hand. A plain gold band glinted on his ring finger. Without having to inspect its inner rim, she knew the words From Sunny, and their wedding date, would not be engraved there. This band was much wider than the one she had given him.

"I leased them from a jeweler," he said.

Sunny shifted her gaze to the road ahead of them. Why should she feel let down that he hadn't kept their wedding bands, ten years after their divorce? She had given hers back to him, hadn't she? She couldn't blame him for disposing of it, along with his. They meant nothing to either of them now.

Striving for indifference, Sunny shoved the new, ornate band onto her ring finger.

The cellular phone rang. Ryan answered with his usual brief greeting. "Yes?" Surprise entered into his voice. "Sunny Shannon? Yes, she is."

Sunny quickly took the phone from him, certain that an emergency had arisen at the hotel. "This is Sunny."

Ryan watched as the anxiety on her face changed into one of mild annoyance—although a distinct twinkle of affection lightened her expressive green eyes. "Hello, Grandma."

He *thought* he'd recognized Olive's cantankerous voice.

"The man who answered?" said Sunny uneasily. "He's, uh, a business associate of mine." Ryan recognized the tone of Sunny's voice, too; she was evading a point. "You thought it sounded like who?" She laughed a little too boisterously. "Ryan! What in heaven's name would Ryan be doing with *me*?"

Her eyes met his in a silent apology. At least, he hoped it was an apology. She certainly owed him one. Her tone had left no doubt that she considered his presence in her life nothing less than absurd. And why did she feel the need to lie about him to her grandmother?

"I'm on a business trip, Grandma," she explained, "with a very well-respected business associate of mine." Her mouth tightened as she listened. "Now, don't start that again. I can take care of myself." Sunny rolled her eyes. "For Pete's sake, Grandma, I'm twenty-eight years old, not eighteen. Calm down. Have you taken your heart medication today?"

At Sunny's expression of concern and annoyance, Ryan guessed, "She's having one of her spasms."

Sunny nodded. Ryan felt confident that Olive would survive this latest "spasm" just as she had survived the others over the past twenty years, but Sunny seemed genuinely worried.

The urge to put his arm around her—to comfort her, to take her mind off useless worry—nearly overpowered him. It would be so easy, so natural, to pull her against him, whisper some assurance in her ear, inhale the lily fragrance of her hair that shimmered like the finest gold....

He conquered the impulse. He was no fool.

As she made brief replies into the receiver, Ryan stared straight ahead at the road. He could clearly imagine the conversation. Olive's distrust of strange men in the vicinity of her granddaughter bordered on obsession. Her daughter—Sunny's mother—had been "lured away at the tender age of sixteen by some fast-talking city slicker con man," as Olive always told it, and "started on the road to ruin." As far as Olive was concerned, strange men were sent from the devil to corrupt her "innocent young'uns."

Ironic, thought Ryan, that Sunny had "gotten into trouble" with him—a boy she had grown up with. Thank God they'd been married before Olive learned of Sunny's pregnancy, or their wedding might have been conducted at the point of Olive's shotgun.

After another silent moment, Sunny raised her hand in defeat. "Okay, Grandma, okay. Yes, I promise. Now, go take your medication. Goodbye." She hung up the phone, took a moment to regain her composure, then expelled her breath as if she had just climbed a mountain.

"Why did you lie to her about me?"

"I didn't actually lie," Sunny hedged, looking guilty. "You *are* a business associate of mine. And I didn't say you weren't here—I simply asked her what you'd be doing with me."

"Something of a technicality, wouldn't you say?"

"Oh, Ryan, I couldn't tell her you were with me! She really would have had a spasm then. The big one."

Ryan frowned. "Since when does Olive distrust *me*?"

Sunny bit her bottom lip, hesitating. "Since our divorce."

Ryan stared at her. "*You* divorced *me*. How could she blame me for that?"

"You know how she always blames everything on men."

"That's ridiculous."

"Of course it is. We both know it, so there's no use talking about it anymore."

Ryan wanted to probe deeper into the subject, bothered more by Olive's bad opinion of him than he would ever admit. From the closed, stubborn expression on Sunny's face, though, he knew she'd say no more. He supposed he'd have to confront Olive face-to-face, once his business at Windsong Place had been settled.

"Besides," said Sunny, "I don't want her to know about this deal we're working on. I haven't told her we'd be anywhere near Heaven's Hollow or Windsong Place. If the deal doesn't go through, she'd be terribly disappointed. I'd rather wait and surprise her with my new position when it's a sure thing."

Ryan nodded. He'd have it no other way. They drove in silence for a few miles until another question occurred to him. "What did Olive make you promise?"

A becoming blush stole into Sunny's cheeks. "She always worries when I go on the road with male business associates."

"I gathered that." He actually couldn't blame Olive for that particular worry—he himself didn't like the thought of Sunny traveling around with men, either. And she wasn't even his concern. "So what did you promise her?"

"To lock my hotel door at night."

He was about to say "Good advice." But then he remembered that Olive had been talking about *this* business trip. And of course, that advice wouldn't apply. They'd be sharing a room.

Ryan's hands tightened around the steering wheel. That aspect of the situation hadn't fully hit him before. But it did now, like a heavyweight champion's jab to his gut. Sunny would be spending the nights in his room.

As if her thoughts were traveling down the same disconcerting path, the silence between them suddenly hummed with tension. Ryan chanced a glance in her direction; she looked as unnerved as he.

"I assume we can arrange for a two-room suite?" she ventured. "You know, with a sleeper sofa in the living room? We can say we need the extra room for your work space."

"Of course."

They both breathed easier with this plan firmly in place.

AFTER THEY'D TURNED NORTH on the Blue Ridge Parkway, the terrain had grown more mountainous; the slopes and curves of the two-lane highway more dramatic; the elevation higher. The air blew fresher and cooler through the open windows, scented with spring grasses and mountain laurel.

Ryan's ears blocked with the altitude, and his occasional glances over the sharp precipice to his right afforded him mild, pleasurable rushes of vertigo. He had once known every curve of these mountain roads. He'd been gone too long. Ten years.

He veered westward off the parkway. Pines, oaks and poplars grew tall and majestic on hillsides, then twisted and sideways on vertical slopes. Colorful wildflowers laced the greenery. Crystal streams trickled down russet boulders, gleaming silver in the afternoon sunshine.

They crossed the Honeysuckle Gorge Bridge. He remembered skipping stones across the French Broad River that gurgled and sang below them. And pushing a laughing, bare-legged Sunny into its gray-green waters on hot summer days.

Ryan slowed the car in anticipation of a hidden turn. Before long, he came to the sign reading Windsong Place. Next Left.

Sunny whispered, "We're here," as if entering a church.

He turned the wheel sharply and ascended a steep drive.

And then Windsong Place appeared. Grand and imposing, the Victorian mansion dominated the entire mountaintop, facing east toward the river. Fluted chimneys, projecting turrets and a multitude of gables rose in graceful angles against a backdrop of smoky blue mountain peaks. The mansion's once-weathered exterior now gleamed a sunshine yellow, trimmed in cool forest green. The expansive verandas and wraparound front porch with slender columns were brilliantly reconstructed.

Ryan had never seen Windsong Place looking more splendid. And never had he felt more like a stranger at its threshold.

He drove past blossoming dogwoods and redbud trees. A young couple strolled through carpets of daisies; a man and a boy carried fishing gear toward the river. Guests, he presumed.

How odd to see strangers here. When he'd been a boy, his father had never entertained. The only people to enjoy this land, other than he himself, had been employees. And his pal, Grady Barrett, whose father owned the adjacent property. But Grady had stayed with his divorced father only every other weekend. Which left Ryan alone most of the time. With Sunny, of course.

As Ryan rounded a curve in the drive, Sunny cried, "Ryan, stop the car. Stop! Now!" She was gazing out her passenger window into the forest.

Ryan immediately steered off the concrete drive and applied his emergency brake to stop the car from rolling back down the incline. Only when Sunny flashed him a purely mischievous smile and opened her door did Ryan realize she was *not* about to get sick. She was merely up to something.

Mystified, Ryan switched off the motor and followed her into the woods. In her white eyelet peasant blouse and brightly colored layered skirt, with gold hoops sparkling at her ears and playfulness in her steps, she looked like a gypsy luring him to her caravan.

"Look," she urged, pointing at a granite boulder shaped like a huge Indian arrowhead. "Remember this?"

Ryan stared at the boulder for a moment. Without answering, he paced into the woods—ten long strides, at an exact right angle from the point of the rock. To his immediate left was an oak tree. And neck-high—actually, waist-high to him now—was a small round opening in the tree trunk.

Tagging along at his elbow, Sunny grinned delightedly. "Go ahead. See if there's any messages for you."

He frowned at her. She was studying the knothole in the tree with intense interest, nearly holding her breath, her hands clasped in front of her as if she expected him to pull out a treasure.

Ryan peered into the hole. When he was sure no living creature had made its nest inside, he reached in. Suddenly, as if a mighty vacuum had sucked him in, Ryan slammed against the tree trunk, his entire hand swallowed into the bowels of the tree, clear up to his forearm. "Aaaahhh!" he yelled.

Startled, Sunny screamed in alarm, grabbed hold of his forearm and yanked with all her might. "What is it, Ry? What is it?" she cried, tugging and tugging, to no avail. His body shook spasmodically beside her, deepening her panic.

Until she managed to pull his hand free from the tree. And she realized he was shaking with laughter.

"Oh!" she gasped, staring at him in utter disdain. "You scared the pie-doodle out of me." She dropped his forearm disgustedly. Ryan leaned his shoulder against the tree for support, racked with uncontrollable mirth.

"You! You—!" Unable to think of a word foul enough to describe him, she slugged him in the shoulder.

Which only set him off into a fresh bout of laughter.

"That's it. I'm going back to the car." As she stalked away in a fit of mock indignation—her own traitorous lips threatening to twitch into a smile any moment—Ryan lagged behind her, his laughter winding down as he wiped his streaming eyes with the back of his hand.

"Got to watch out for those tree goblins," he warned.

"Shut up." She reached the car and slung open the door. Before she could slide into the passenger seat, he grabbed her arm and firmly turned her around to face him.

"How did you know about that knothole, anyway? That was Grady's and my secret message place."

"I followed you."

Ryan stared at her appraisingly. "Did you ever take any of our messages?"

"Of course not. I read a few, though."

Ryan shook his head in stern disapproval.

"Well, I didn't have anyone to send messages to *me*."

"You—" he tapped his index finger beneath her collarbone "—were a girl." Sure he'd made his point, he left her standing at the open passenger door and rounded the front of his car.

"So?" she called across the car roof, her tone emphatic, sarcastic and reminiscent of the brat who'd tagged around after him every summer.

"So," he explained with great patience, "you were too busy fooling around with Betty Sue."

"Betty Lou," Sunny corrected him. Her eyes then widened in surprise. "You remembered her!"

Embarrassed, he muttered, "How can I forget? You dragged that doll around with you everywhere."

Sunny laughed, leaning her forearms on the roof of his sports car. "Remember when we played cops and robbers, and you had to tie up Betty Lou, too? Toughest outlaw you ever brought to justice."

"*I* was the outlaw. You never could get that straight." Ryan slid into the car and slammed the door.

Sunny did the same. "You were the good guy. So was I."

"Girls," he uttered in mock disgust as he started the engine. "You even brought that doll with you during storms."

"Of course. She needed protection, too."

Ryan fell silent as he steered the car up the driveway, remembering. During thunderstorms, the wind whipping around the house's peaks and gables whistled and hummed like an eerie song. Ryan felt certain the house had been named for this peculiarity. But to two children alone in their separate beds late at night, the wind sounded more like supernatural wailing than a song.

Sunny would sneak into his bed whenever the winds began to sing, afraid of the mansion's ghost. They'd fall asleep together, he and she, listening to the house's eerie music.

"You were the one who told me about the ghost in the first place," Sunny said, in perfect timing with his thoughts.

"The ghost of the mountain climber who died on Devil's Ridge." Ryan grinned. It had been his best story. And based on pure fact. A man *had* died trying to climb Devil's Ridge. And there had been times that Ryan had felt a ghostly presence in the shadowy corridors of the house.

Those had been the innocent days. Those days he could share his bed with Sunny and not think about anything but ghosts.

Parking the car in the circular front drive, Ryan took a moment to gaze at her. Her sunny, chin-length curls were wind-ruffled now, the gold hoop earrings glittering among them. Her dimple played merrily beside her smile.

In ten years, he hadn't laughed as hard as he had today.

He had missed her friendship. Unnerved by the realization, Ryan switched off the motor and muttered gruffly, "Let's go check into a double suite." And he led the way up the flight of stairs that rose through a fragrant pink azalea garden to the wide, white-columned front porch.

An elderly couple emerged from the inn carrying croquet mallets and headed across a small paved parking lot.

Ryan paused, staring at that parking lot. Open grass had once stretched there. Sunny had pitched him baseballs on it. And he'd thrown her a few football passes. Tackled her. Kissed her beneath that canopy of ancient oaks until they'd both been quaking with the need for more. . . .

"Want to go explore?" Her voice was soft as a mountain breeze.

"No," he replied brusquely. "I'm ready to go inside."

The camaraderie between them had somehow changed; he no longer wanted to reminisce. Without waiting to see if she followed, he strode to the front entrance.

At the massive, polished oak door, an inexplicable urge overtook him. Slowly he turned and stared out over the sloping front lawn toward the long, winding drive that disappeared into a sea of treetops.

A bewildering emotion gripped him. A sudden sadness, a hollow ache. A haunting sense of loss.

He scoffed at himself. He hadn't lived here for ten years. Why should he feel the loss so keenly now? His home was his New York apartment. Or his London flat. But neither place seemed even remotely deserving of the title "home."

Gradually he became aware of the woman who stood beside him, gazing up into his face with a troubled look of her own. "It's the porch, isn't it?"

His brows drew together as he tried to make sense of Sunny's words. "The porch?"

"It always did upset you. No matter how happy you were, your mood always soured when you stepped out here."

"My mood's not soured," he replied with mild mockery. But as he thought back, he realized he never *had* spent much time out here, although comfortable rockers had always lined the shady porch. With a dismissive shake of his head, Ryan turned away from the view of the front drive that disturbed him even now.

He would concentrate only on the business aspect of his visit—not on his emotional reaction to it. He wanted Windsong Place; it was his birthright. And he would do anything to stop his father from taking it away from him again.

MUTED VOICES could be heard from the dining room that lay just beyond the front parlor on their right. But the spacious Oak Hall, which comprised the heart of the house, was blessedly empty of strangers as Sunny and Ryan ambled through it.

Sunny wished she could read Ryan's thoughts. His gray eyes remained coolly impassive, his strong jaw determinedly squared, as he surveyed the twelve-foot ceilings with exposed oak beams and the walls of native oak paneling polished to a warm, rich glow. He said not a word as he walked across the familiar burgundy, mauve and gray Oriental carpet that still decorated the dark oak floor. Potted ferns and freshly cut roses perfumed the air, just as they had in years past, along with the scent of furniture polish.

The familiar ambience of the place transported Sunny back through the years, to a time when she belonged here. Glancing toward the entrance foyer, she clearly remembered.

She hadn't been dressed as a bride; she had worn no long bridal gown, no lace veil. Only a simple white sundress, a single strand of pearls and fresh orange blossoms in her hair. But when she descended the Grand Staircase, Ryan's eyes had made her feel beautiful.

They were married in Asheville, then returned directly to Windsong Place. Her groom—strong, handsome and vibrant—had carried her across the threshold.

"Welcome home, Mrs. Alexander." He had breathed the words in a triumphant whisper against her hair; a whisper underscored with anticipation, for they were young and ruled by a passionate physical need for each other.

The house was exclusively theirs for the night. The staff was off; his father was residing in his New York City town house. They were entirely alone.

Ryan had whirled her through the great Oak Hall, around and around, until they collapsed, dizzy and laughing, into the winged armchair beside the immense fireplace.

With kisses that stoked a feverish longing, he had unclothed her, item by item, until she wore only the strand of pearls. They had made love there, for the first time as husband and wife, on the Oriental carpet in front of the hearth, beneath the huge oil painting of his great-grandfather in its gilded frame above the mantel.

Sunny diverted her gaze from the hearth; the memories were too strong and vital. And she noticed that Ryan, too, was staring at the hearth.

She carefully avoided his eyes. The idea that he might be remembering that same time in their lives played havoc with her serenity. She concentrated instead on the portrait of a stoic-looking Victorian gentleman that now hung above the mantel. A stranger to them, of course.

Sunny wandered toward the foot of the Grand Staircase, where the ceiling rose to a startling height of thirty-two feet. Bordered by hand-turned spool balusters with a stacked-bead effect, the staircase ascended from the rear quarter of the Oak Hall and turned several times on its way to the upper floors.

Three stained-glass windows above the oak staircase admitted a colorful stream of muted light that illuminated the stairwell like mystical rays from heaven.

The effect, as always, was dazzling. And again, transported Sunny back through time, to when they had climbed this stairway together....

Another topic she'd avoid.

"Mr. and Mrs. Alexander?"

Momentarily confused by the salutation—almost as if the past had suddenly come to life—Sunny whirled from her private musing to face a portly woman with graying hair and a maternal smile in her almond brown eyes.

Ryan stepped forward and smoothly introduced himself and Sunny—as Mr. and Mrs. Alexander, of course.

A false title, she reminded herself. Just as it had been ten years ago. But despite that knowledge, the introduction infused Sunny with an illogical rush of pleasure.

"Welcome to Windsong Place. I am Mrs. Lee, the assistant innkeeper. Mr. and Mrs. Tanner have been detained in town for the evening. But they will be back tomorrow morning. They'd like you to join them for breakfast on their veranda. Seven o'clock, if that's okay with you. For now, please step to the registration desk and I will give you your keys."

They trailed Mrs. Lee past a chattering group of middle-aged couples carrying blankets and picnic baskets to the registration desk that had been built in the small room beyond the Oak Hall, where a music room had once been. It seemed irreverent to Sunny, building something as commercial as a reception area in Windsong Place.

She had to remind herself of the purpose of her visit—to obtain the manager's position. This reception area and the office behind it would undoubtedly be her base of operation.

"We'd like a double suite," said Ryan, not visibly affected by the practical renovations. "I'll be working late on my paperwork, and I'd rather not disturb my wife's sleep."

Dismay creased Mrs. Lee's forehead. "I'm sorry, sir, but our only double suite is occupied. Mrs. Tanner has already reserved a suite in your name."

"Can't we reserve two suites, then?" suggested Sunny hopefully. "That way Ryan can use one as a workroom, while I . . ."

"We are filled to capacity for a private wedding being held this evening in the ballroom, ma'am. Besides, Mrs. Tanner very specifically reserved this particular suite for you." Mrs. Lee looked quickly around, as if to be sure no one else was listening, then said in an undertone, "She even made a young couple move to another suite so you could have this one. She was very excited about arranging this for you."

A terrible foreboding filled Sunny.

"I'm sure we'll be happy with any room Mrs. Tanner reserved for us," Ryan assured her. Mrs. Lee handed him and Sunny each a key and gave directions to the room.

Upon hearing the location of the suite, a blush crept into Sunny's cheeks. She sensed Ryan stiffen beside her. They did not look at each other.

Ryan broke the silence between them by clearing his throat. "Maybe you'd like to tour the grounds before we . . . go upstairs?"

"Yes, yes, a tour of the grounds would be fine."

"And afterward, we can try out the restaurant."

"Wonderful idea."

Neither mentioned the specter that loomed bright and mocking between them. For the suite that Lavinia had booked in their name—third floor, last room on the right—was the very room they had occupied as husband and wife.

5

THEY WANDERED THROUGH the rose gardens, the apple orchard and the gazebo overlooking the river, engaging in meaningless small talk about the minute changes they could detect in the landscaping, but darkness finally forced them inside.

They shared what should have been a leisurely supper of freshly caught mountain trout, served in the dining room, complete with candlelight and piano music. Both of their plates remained virtually untouched. Nevertheless, they ordered a sinfully rich French chocolate silk pie—left mostly uneaten—until neither of them could think of a single reason not to climb that Grand Staircase to the room awaiting them on the third floor.

They did so in tense silence.

Sunny fumbled with her key and slowly pushed open the glossy wooden door. Ryan stood behind her, surveying the room.

Gentle, golden lamplight illuminated the cozy suite that time had done little to change. The same oak-manteled fireplace stretched along one wall, opposite the set of French doors that led to a veranda. The hardwood floor was adorned with the same Oriental rug in front of the gray stone hearth. And the same blue-patterned wallpaper with pink Victorian cabbage-rose trim decorated the room.

"It's the same," Sunny whispered. "Like it was yesterday."

Ryan glanced at her, and the thought rushed through him: she was more of his yesterday than any of it. She was his yesterday.

"And soon it will all be yours again," she said.

Except *she* wouldn't be his. The thought sprang upon him unbidden, and he struggled to banish it. Nostalgia. It was only nostalgia.

He watched her move around in her new, efficient manner, slender and lovely in her white eyelet blouse and gypsy skirt. She opened the two large, wood-framed windows and the set of French doors, allowing a crosscurrent of fresh mountain breezes to stir the lace draperies.

A spring-scented gust playfully riffled tendrils of her hair across her cheeks. He watched her breathe deeply of the cool mountain fragrance he remembered so well.

But it wasn't the mountain breeze that filled his senses. It was the sight of her here, in this room, with her honey-smooth skin and emerald eyes and golden hair illuminated by lamplight. He remembered the texture of that hair—warm, fragrant silk in his fingers—and he wanted to touch it again.

Shaken by the strength of the impulse, he looked away from her, then moved away from her, putting a good distance between them. Nostalgia, he told himself. Damn nostalgia.

For something to do, he wandered beneath the small archway into the tiny dressing room with a closet on one side and an antique mirrored vanity table on the other. On the far end was the crystal-handled door of the adjoining bathroom.

Peering inside, he saw that the bathroom remained basically unchanged. Sprigs of flowers decorated the wallpaper; gray-and-white tiles formed a pattern on the floor.

An oval walnut-framed mirror topped a pedestal sink. It was immaculate.

His attention was caught by the claw-footed tub in one corner—a Victorian original—and the glassed-in shower stall across from it. He had shared both with his bride. Memories flooded back, as clear as Carolina mountain air. Shampoo fragrance. Steamy kisses. Green eyes, dark with passion. Soap-lathered skin. Sunny, wet and naked against him...

Heat washed through him, and an inner voice warned, *Get her out of here. Out of this house. Out of your life.*

He gritted his teeth. He couldn't. He needed her to reclaim Windsong Place, and it would take more than memories to stop him. He turned to find her watching him from the archway in awkward silence.

"You can have the bed," he muttered hoarsely. "All I need is a pillow and blanket on the floor." He saw the hesitation in her green eyes before she veiled them beneath dark gold lashes. And vividly he recalled another time she had hesitated with similar self-consciousness within this very bedroom.

The night he had finally made love to her, after torturous weeks of superhuman restraint, stopping just at the brink. They hadn't even considered marriage yet; he'd had only one thing on his mind. He'd brought her here deliberately, to the most appealing room in the house, covertly, in the dead of night, with candles, flowers and wine. And with every intention of seducing her, taking her virginity.

He had succeeded.

The unwanted warmth again rose within him. His gaze, restless and needful, lowered to her mouth, and he wondered what would happen now if he kissed her....

"I suppose I don't have much choice but to let you have your way," she capitulated softly.

In the space of a missed heartbeat, his chest expanded; his breath caught and his arousal hardened. But he soon realized she was referring to his use of the floor as a bed. Not a sampling of her mouth. Her body.

He brushed past her, unable to bear her nearness another moment. She moved away as he grabbed their suitcases from beside the doorway where the bellman had earlier deposited them and slung them onto the luggage rack of the dressing room.

"Are you sure you don't mind...sleeping on the floor?" she called from the far end of the suite.

He turned briskly around to stare at her. Hope drummed in his ears. Was she offering a place beside her in bed?

"I mean, I wouldn't mind camping out down there," she added hurriedly.

Disgruntled by his dashed hopes, Ryan muttered, "I said I'd take the floor and I will. End of subject."

That damned renegade dimple flashed again in her cheek. "Here," she said softly. "Maybe this will help." She tossed a small patchwork quilt across an armchair.

He recognized the quilt. It was the one he had bought her at a mountain fair, ten long years ago. His first gift to her. They had used it that entire summer to lie together in the warm summer grass...in private places, where her grandmother, or other workers, would never think of looking.

Intently he searched her eyes.

"It's...warm," she whispered defensively. "And... and...I know how cold this house can get at night. Even in May."

He supposed he could take her explanation at face value. She certainly needed no other reason to keep the quilt for ten years, or to bring it with her now.

But woven into its fabric, along with the patchwork colors, were memories much warmer than the quilt could ever be. And Ryan swore he could read those memories in her eyes, in the quiver of her lip, in the heat of her beguiling blush.

A fierce gladness swept through him. After all was said and done, it was his quilt she snuggled under, his house she'd be living in, his ghost she'd be sleeping with.

His gaze thoroughly possessed her, if only for a moment.

Drawing in a breath, Ryan forced himself to look away. *You can't have her. You don't even want her. She's Trouble with a capital* T.

But later, as he lay on the hardwood floor softened only by a thin throw rug and Sunny's patchwork quilt, he couldn't help wondering what it was—if anything—she felt for him.

A SLEEKLY MUSCLED ARM crossed between Sunny's breasts and drew her tightly against the warm, hard male body behind her.

"Mmmmm," she purred. And snuggled closer.

A masculine groan near her ear spread a pleasurable tingle throughout her. She pressed her languorous body intimately against his and delighted in the immediate hardening of his muscles, his tightened embrace.

He nestled her breast in the palm of his hand.

A wonderfully wicked heat flowed through her. As she moved her hips in sensuous rotation, she became aware that her cotton nightgown had ridden up to her thighs, and her bare legs were entwined with powerful, muscle-corded ones.

Not for a second, even in that hazy half dream, did Sunny wonder who the man was, or how he had gotten there. Only one man ever held her in her dreams. Only one man ever made her want in this primal, earthy way....

The buzz of the telephone jolted Sunny to full wakefulness. Her eyes flew open. What was she doing? She was *in bed* with Ryan! Frantically she disengaged herself from his embrace. Nearly falling out of bed, she switched on the bedside lamp and turned around to glare at him.

He was fast asleep.

Trembling, she answered the buzzing phone. Wake-up call. She glanced at the bedside clock. Almost six. Hanging up the receiver, she whirled around and shoved Ryan's sinewy, bronzed shoulder. In quiet fury, she demanded, "Get up!"

His eyes slowly opened and he squinted at her. "What the hell—?" His smooth, muscular chest was bare, his slim lower body tangled in the bedcovers.

"What do you think you're doing in this bed?"

Ryan propped himself up on one elbow and dragged his palm down his dark, beard-shadowed face. "Somethin' wrong?"

"You said you'd sleep on the floor!"

He frowned at her. "That floor is hell. And the damned armchair isn't any better." Lying back against the pillows, he closed his eyes and hoarsely pleaded, "Come back to bed, Sunny."

Disconcerted by his sleep-husky invitation that sounded so dangerously alluring, Sunny stood by the bedside, nonplussed, watching him doze off. "Not on your life," she vowed.

After a second or two, his eyes reopened. All vestiges of sleep were gone. His glance slowly descended the length of her—with an awareness that tingled everywhere his eyes touched. And although her sherbert-green nightgown was not precisely sheer, she could feel her nipples straining against the thin cotton. She crossed her arms over her breasts and glared.

"Are you saying that I . . . *did* . . . something to you?" he asked, his voice just above a whisper as his eyes again met hers.

She lifted her chin, hoping he couldn't see her pulse pounding in her throat. "As a matter of fact, you did."

He stared at her in disbelief. She blushed warmly.

He cursed, threw the covers off and paced across the hardwood floor away from her. She realized he wore maroon silk pajama bottoms. He had not been, as she'd imagined, naked beneath those covers. Pacing back toward her, he demanded, "What'd I do?"

She shook her head and reached for her robe, which lay draped over the armchair.

"Sunny, would you please tell me what the hell I did?"

"I'd rather not discuss it."

He sat down heavily on the bed and plowed his fingers through his unruly hair. "I'm sorry, Sunny. Damn it all to hell, I'm sorry." He looked stricken. "I swear I was asleep. I never intended to . . . to do anything."

His eyes met hers, and she saw brutal self-recrimination in his gaze. The sincerity and depth of it surprised her. He was just as determined as she to prevent their involvement. The thought should have comforted her, but it didn't. It made her feel colder than the draft swirling across the hardwood floor.

"Forget it," she mumbled, slipping into her terry bathrobe as she headed for the privacy of the bathroom. A rather silly thing for her to have said, she realized. He couldn't very well forget something he hadn't consciously experienced.

CASUALLY DRESSED in jeans, soft leather boots and a chambray shirt, Ryan walked out through the French doors onto the small veranda, leaned his forearms on the wrought-iron rail and gazed at the sun rising over the smoky Blue Ridge Mountains. Its crimson-and-gold beauty had never failed to captivate him. But even the mountain sunrise didn't offer him the distraction he sorely needed this Saturday morning.

Mentally, he cursed himself. He hadn't meant to touch her. The last thing they needed now was a misunderstanding. This was a business venture, and no matter how much he had to struggle against his baser instincts, he meant to keep his relationship with Sunny professional.

He moved slightly and winced at the soreness in his back. Last night on the hardwood floor had been as bad as he'd described it—pure hell. But even worse than the physical discomfort had been the knowledge that only a few feet from him, Sunny lay in that damned bed. The sight of her there had fired his imagination. And his memory. Every passionate interlude they'd ever shared in that bed had come back to taunt him.

The night had been hell. Pure hell.

Ryan supposed he should have toughed it out on the floor. But at five o'clock this morning, he'd had as much as he could take. He'd climbed into the bed, careful not to disturb her. And once he had mastered the nearly overwhelming impulse to pull her slender, lush body against his, he had finally slept.

And then, to be awakened by an angry woman accusing him of sexual misconduct . . . Ryan shook his head. He couldn't have done much in five minutes. At least, not in his sleep.

What *had* he done?

Just imagining the possibilities returned his body to the same state he'd been in half the night. Why did she affect him so? Hormones. Damned hormones.

The door to the suite opened and Sunny stepped out onto the veranda with him. He continued to stare off into the distance.

In a voice as brisk as the morning air, she said, "Compliments of the house."

He cocked an eye in her direction as she set down steaming coffee and a newspaper on the table. She then strolled to the other end of the veranda to stare at the sunrise.

She wore neat, tight jeans and a dusty rose sweater that delineated every alluring curve. Ryan stifled a groan. Her eyes were too enticingly green this morning, and her mouth too kissable. Memories reeled of happier mornings spent on this veranda. God, how he had loved kissing her....

Ryan grunted his thanks as he picked up the aromatic coffee. The sun had crowned the mountains in a blaze of golden glory, birds twittered in the trees, hornets buzzed in the nearby garden and the breeze whispered its own regrets through the forest's shining leaves.

As if forcing the words, Sunny admitted, "I understand your difficulty in sleeping on the hardwood floor. I'm sure it was terribly uncomfortable. And I accept some of the blame for...what happened." She sounded truly contrite.

His curiosity piqued, he searched her face. "Why?"

A delicate flush tinted her cheeks. "For not realizing immediately..." Her flustered words halted, and she averted her face.

Had she responded to his advances? Ryan clenched his teeth. How could he have slept through it?

"What I'm trying to say is—" She finally worked up the nerve to look him in the eye. "I believe you were not aware of your actions when you...put your arm around me."

"Put my arm around you?" he repeated. "That's all I did?" Too late, he realized he sounded disappointed.

Fortunately, she didn't seem to notice. She was too busy taking offense at his trivializing of the incident. "No, as a matter of fact," she snapped, "it wasn't *all* you did. Your hands were in places they had no business being."

Ryan took a quick gulp of hot coffee to stop from asking for more specifics—just to hear her describe them. Instead, he let his imagination run wild. He simply couldn't help it. "Well let me lay your mind to rest, Ms. Shannon," he said, emphasizing her maiden name with a resentment he couldn't quite suppress. "I have no designs of any kind on your body."

Again, her cheeks flooded with color. Her eyes sparkled with an emotion he couldn't quite identify.

Ruthlessly, he continued, "You are my employee. And regardless of our past history, or our present mission, I intend to keep this venture strictly professional. If I *did* make advances to you in my sleep last night—"

"You mean you doubt it?"

"I didn't say that."

"Good." She turned her gaze toward the mountains again. "Then I accept your apology."

Although he hadn't actually been offering an apology, he nodded, glad that she was willing to put the episode behind them. "I'll drive into Heaven's Hollow today and pick up a fold-up cot. We'll stash it behind the luggage in the closet so the maids won't wonder why we're sleeping separately. All we need is a rumor to reach Lavinia that we're not getting along."

"Great idea." The relief in her eyes spoke volumes. It shouldn't have bothered him at all.

He drained his coffee, set the mug down on the outdoor table and made up his mind that he'd be just as relieved as she that they no longer had to share a bed.

ON THE VERANDA of the Tanners' private suite, they were served a breakfast of hot muffins, fresh fruit and smoky, sizzling sausage links. Lavinia, however, was not present.

"She's busy with the group from last night's wedding." Wilbur's amiable smile was almost hidden beneath his heavy white mustache. "We extend personal attention to every party who stays with us. She'll be back shortly." He chuckled. "She's looking forward to seeing your plans for the week, Sunny."

Sunny hoped Lavinia would approve of the activities she had planned. From the brochures she had picked up at the registration desk, she realized the inn currently sponsored very little in the way of entertainment: a croquet court, hiking trails and a pianist in the restaurant. A nice start, but not enough.

Sunny remembered her girlhood dreams of entertaining here as the lady of the house, with the freedom to endow her guests with all the splendor these North Carolina mountains had to give. She would use some of those girlhood dreams now.

The telephone rang inside Wilbur's suite and he excused himself to answer it. Ryan took the opportunity to ask Sunny, "Do you have everything you need for the week's activities?"

"Almost."

"Almost? What's missing?"

Sunny smiled wryly. "Horses. I would have liked to fill the stables again and ride the trails, like we used to when we were kids. But it would have been ridiculously expensive to have the horses shipped in for a week. We'd have to hire someone to care for them, and for the stables."

After Wilbur returned, they ate a leisurely breakfast, enjoying the gentle May sunshine. Wilbur finally broke the idyllic silence. "I might as well warn you—" he paused to spear a sausage "—there's a problem we'll need to settle before Lavinia will sign the purchase agreement."

Ryan lowered his fork from his mouth and stared at Wilbur questioningly. "What problem?"

To Sunny's amazement, a flush of embarrassment deepened the natural redness of Wilbur's cheeks. He took a moment to swallow his sausage. "How long you two been married?"

Ryan and Sunny met each other's eyes, waiting for the other to answer. Biting the proverbial bullet, Sunny replied, "Two years."

"Six months," said Ryan at the exact same moment. A deafening silence followed.

Sunny broke it with a nervous laugh. "Actually, we've dated for two years, and have been married for six months."

Wilbur looked more uncomfortable than ever.

"Is there a problem with that?" demanded Ryan.

"Could be."

Sunny's stomach flip-flopped. Ryan's eyes darkened. Had their charade been uncovered? Had the Tanners learned they weren't married?

Wilbur set down his fork and pushed his near-empty plate away. "I thought about keeping my mouth shut and letting Lavinia handle this, since she's the one who's so darned worried. But I can't see springing something like this on a couple as nice as you without a warning."

"A warning?" repeated Sunny, bracing herself.

"Get to the point, Wilbur." Ryan's abruptness drew Sunny's admonishing gaze.

Wilbur just chuckled. "I don't blame you for getting impatient, son. Never liked jumping through hoops myself." From the pocket of his country-club shirt, he drew a cigar and lit it. "As you know, Lavinia is determined to sell the inn to a happily married couple. Mom and pop and apple pie . . ."

"We discussed all that Friday," cut in Ryan. "I thought Lavinia had approved of us."

"At the time, she did. But she went to the beauty parlor and her stylist mentioned seeing you, Ryan, in a tabloid." He hesitated again with an uncomfortable glance at Sunny. "Maybe I should talk to you about this in private."

"There's nothing you could say that Sunny can't hear."

Sunny nodded her encouragement.

"Okay, then." He lifted his hands in a here-goes-nothing gesture. "I'm sure you can imagine how important marital fidelity is to Lavinia. There's nothing that upsets her more than men fooling around on their wives, or vice versa."

"What does that have to do with—"

Wilbur raised a hand to silence a visibly annoyed Ryan. "Just two months ago, there was an article about you. It seems you were . . . uh . . . on a yacht with . . ."

Sunny surprised both men with a gentle laugh. "I'll bet I know what you're going to say." She hoped her cheerfulness didn't sound too forced.

"What?" said both men in unison.

"Princess Catherine, right?"

Ryan's brows drew together, but Wilbur exhaled in relief. "Guess you read the article."

"Read it? I was *in* it," declared Sunny. Wilbur gaped at her, as did Ryan. "Of course, they never mentioned *my* name," she said, piqued. "Makes the story much more interesting if the readers believe Ryan is doing something illicit."

"I know just how those news folks can be," Wilbur commiserated.

"Damned media," cursed Ryan.

"In fact, they didn't even get my face quite in focus. But if you take a magnifying glass and look closely, you might be able to see me there behind Ryan."

After digesting that piece of information in silence, Wilbur asked with sudden interest, "So you two know Princess Catherine?"

"Barely at all," demurred Ryan, while Sunny claimed, "A close, personal friend."

Wilbur puffed happily on his cigar. "Well, that clears up *my* questions." Nevertheless his forehead was wrinkled in worry. "Hope Lavinia buys it."

Sunny saw a muscle clench in Ryan's jaw and knew he was reaching the limit of his patience. Quickly, she said, "I'd be happy to talk to Lavinia about it. I was upset myself when that article came out. They took a perfectly innocent social occasion and made Ryan seem like some kind of . . . playboy." She cast him a glance. "A libertine. A womanizer. The worst kind of Don Juan . . ."

"I think we get the point," Ryan muttered.

Sunny smiled sweetly at him. A little too sweetly.

"You two just be yourselves," encouraged Wilbur, "and I'm sure Lavinia will see that you're as happily married as any couple can be." Rising, he gestured with his cigar as if he were a general leading his troops into battle. "Now, let's go downstairs and find her."

"Uh, before we go anywhere, Wilbur," Ryan interjected, "I'd like a copy of the purchase agreement. I'll fax it to my legal department, so we can finalize the sale today."

Wilbur puffed out a cloud of smoke contentedly. "Can't."

"Can't?" repeated Ryan.

"My attorney won't have the contract drawn up until the end of the week." Wilbur smiled paternally beneath his white mustache. "That'll also give you two a chance to convince Lavinia that all is well in paradise."

They found Lavinia in the dining room, where she was ushering a chattering party of guests toward the breakfast buffet. A shame, thought Sunny, that breakfast wasn't served on the glassed-in side porch, where lush plants flourished in the gentle morning sunshine.

She had breakfasted there often with her grandmother. A pleasure she'd never forgotten. She made a mental note to move the breakfast buffet from the dining room to the sun porch.

Lavinia greeted Sunny with smiles and Ryan with a cautious nod that left no doubt she'd be watching him closely.

Sunny felt Ryan's irritation growing; she knew he hated to "perform" for anyone. He'd always set his own goals and never bothered striving to live up to anyone else's expectations. Except his father's, which had been an exercise in futility.

This time, however, he'd asked for it. Their marriage masquerade had been his idea, not hers. She wondered how much his arrogant soul could stand for the sake of Windsong Place.

To her amazement, he pulled her to him with a proprietary arm around her shoulders. "She wants 'happy,'" he whispered against her ear, "we'll show her 'happy.'"

A tremor passed through her at his sudden nearness.

"Wilbur, why don't you take Ryan for a tour or something? Sunny and I have business to discuss."

"The attic," said Ryan immediately. "I'd like to see the attic."

"Nothing up there," replied Wilbur. "Except ghosts." He chuckled at his own humor. Lavinia glared at him. "Just kidding." To Ryan, he mumbled, "We had one staff member who quit because she swore—"

Lavinia interrupted, "Just show him the attic, Wilbur."

Sunny hid a smile. She imagined that the wind blowing through the eaves and gables *would* sound especially eerie in the attic. She hadn't personally been up there. For as long as she could remember, it had lain silent and locked, as if in mute memorial to his late mother, who had used the attic as her piano room, or so Sunny had been told.

After Ryan and Wilbur had left, the two women settled into the private, chintz-decorated parlor adjoining the dining room.

At Lavinia's urging, Sunny handed her the colorful brochure she had designed. The older woman's eyes lit up with approval upon seeing the front of the brochure, which was a watercolor of the mansion and its surrounding mountains.

"Lovely," Lavinia murmured, running her hand reverently over the picture. "Did you paint this?"

Sunny nodded, pleased at her approval. "There are a few activities I didn't include on the brochure," she said, "because I wasn't sure if I could arrange them in time. But generally speaking, this is the game plan."

Lavinia opened the brochure and glanced at the agenda. "My!" she exclaimed. "Oh, my."

Sunny chewed her bottom lip, waiting as Lavinia continued to peruse the list.

Tiny vertical lines gathered between Lavinia's eyebrows. "I'm sure our younger guests would love the whitewater rafting excursion and bathing in the hot springs, but I don't know if Wilbur and I are up to it." She then glanced at Sunny with a definite twinkle in her eyes. "The rest of it, I'm willing to try. When do we start?"

Sunny grinned in relief. "Right now. But our first activity isn't on the agenda."

RYAN DROVE WILBUR'S open-topped Jeep. Wilbur and Lavinia rode in the back seat. Sunny sat in the front beside Ryan. Casually, he slid his arm around her and pulled her closer.

She did her best to pretend it was a common occurrence; one she took for granted, as any wife of long standing would. But sitting there beside him, in the curve of his strong shoulder, inhaling his woodsy, masculine scent, Sunny couldn't imagine ever taking his nearness for granted. She had to remind herself of the reason he was holding her this way—because Lavinia was watching them from the back seat with eagle eyes.

Forcing her mind to function despite the distraction, Sunny gave Ryan directions on how to reach the launch site.

"Launch site?" chimed Wilbur and Lavinia.

Sunny flashed them a "you'll see" smile. "Imagine, if you will, that we are riding in a van—the Windsong Place shuttle— with guests. Ideally, we'd have left the inn before dawn."

Wilbur grunted. Lavinia raised her brows. Ryan slanted Sunny an indulgent glance. Sunny hoped her "guests" would enjoy her surprise.

They drove to the center of a grassy meadow, where yards and yards of rippling, shiny, colorful fabric were attached to a huge basket.

"A hot-air balloon," deduced Lavinia.

Sunny nodded, and Ryan helped her down from the parked Jeep in an absolutely unnecessary gesture of strength. She wished he'd knock it off with the "happiness" routine already.

Resolutely she turned her attention away from his touch, as she eyed the colorful spectacle in the field. Last-minute doubts assailed her. It had sounded so romantic—a hot-air balloon excursion over the mountains, but it was quite another thing to stand in a meadow, about to step into a little basket attached to a balloon.

Yet, anticipation sparkled in Ryan's dove-gray eyes. Again, his arm came around her; this time she welcomed it.

They approached the site where young people in jeans and balloonist T-shirts were milling around. Sunny heard the whir and putter of the inflator fan as it blew air into the deflated balloon, which began to grow like a bubble-gum bubble, slowly at first, until a definite mound took shape.

"It's huge," whispered Sunny, mesmerized. Ryan nodded, watching with interest as the balloon billowed and expanded into a gigantic, smooth sphere.

Looking white around the lips, Lavinia said, "I take it you mean for us to ride in that thing?"

"You don't think it'll be fun?" asked Sunny. From the glance Wilbur and Lavinia exchanged, she realized with a sinking heart that the answer was no. "But you'll be able see the entire mountain and valley."

"We'll watch you enjoy it," Lavinia murmured. "And meet you wherever this thing lands." Grimly, she added, "I hope."

Sunny threw a doubtful glance at Ryan, who watched the balloon inflate. "Maybe we should just skip this activity." She tried to hide her disappointment. As a little girl, she had watched the colorful balloons glide over the mountaintops and she'd fantasized about sailing above Windsong Place some day, when she could afford it.

"Skip the balloon ride?" said Ryan. "Not on your life."

Sunny grinned at his low-key brand of enthusiasm. She'd known he'd be in favor of it. He'd gone many times with his school friends and he'd always described the trip to her.

The hum of the inflator fan stopped and a peaceful silence reclaimed the meadow. Seconds later, with a *whoosh* of the burner, the balloon stood up, proudly erect and graceful.

Wilbur urged, "Go on, you two." Though unwilling to take the trip himself, he seemed eager to watch. Without giving Sunny a chance to decline, Ryan laced his hand through hers and pulled her toward the colorful giant straining to be free.

He conferred in private with one of the men in a balloonist T-shirt, who handed him a walkie-talkie. Afterward, he helped Sunny climb into to the surprisingly sturdy craft made of wicker, rattan and leather. The creaking of the rigging seemed to whisper last-minute warnings.

Ryan climbed in beside her. "Where's the pilot?" she asked in mild alarm.

"You're looking at him."

"They're going to let you fly this thing?"

"Bribery will get you anywhere," he replied with a cocky smile, and Sunny remembered the boy he'd been—showing off some new skill he had mastered, fully expecting her admiration.

The manager of the operation told Ryan the approximate landing target he should aim for, considering the direction and velocity of the wind. He warned Ryan to watch the fuel gauge—he wouldn't want the propane tanks to run dry. And he told him to steer clear of power lines. And to keep in contact via the walkie-talkie with the chasers who would be following in cars. Ryan nodded and pulled on a cord.

With a *whoosh* of the burner, the basket lifted. Flames momentarily heated the air and Sunny was overcome by a strange, buoyant sensation. The small crowd of spectators cheered and waved as the balloon ascended, and the ground dropped away.

The roar of the burner stopped; silence claimed them.

Sunny shut her eyes, feeling as if she might make a fool of herself and panic. Soon, though, nature's music filled her ears: the calling of birds in the treetops, the croaking of frogs below, the gurgling of a mountain brook, the rustling of the wind through the forest.

Ryan wrapped his arms around her from behind as they drifted through the air as smoothly as a cloud. "Open your eyes, Sunny. Look."

She obeyed, and with a soft cry of wonder she saw the treetops drifting by just beneath them. She felt as if she could reach out and touch them with her fingertips. Beyond the trees, the mountainous horizon stretched all around her, sunlight golden and smoky blue. Infinitely peaceful. Beautiful beyond words.

She felt as if she could see into eternity. "It's lovely."

"Didn't I tell you?" He tightened his arms around her, and they sailed on in eloquent silence, awed by the buoyant feeling and the breathtaking scenery passing beneath them.

"Look over there," Ryan directed, leaning against a post on the rim of the basket. "The French Broad River."

"It looks like a sparkling silver ribbon, doesn't it."

"We'll be coming up to Heaven's Hollow soon. You'll know we're near civilization when you hear the dogs."

"The dogs?"

Ryan grinned. "Just listen."

As they came within sight of her grandmother's peaceful community nestled within a green valley, Sunny heard the dogs. First one, then another. Then a chorus of barking and howling.

She laughed at the canine ruckus they were causing below.

"Never fails." Ryan rested his forearm on the leather-topped railing. "Maybe they hear the wind whistling through the balloon." He pointed down to neat little patches of yards. "Olive's log cabin should be down there somewhere."

"I see it! Look, Ry, beyond that grove of trees."

"That's it." In another moment, he said, "Ah. Now we're getting somewhere. Devil's Ridge."

Sunny peered down at the dangerous gray-and-russet rocky cliff that overlooked a river gorge.

"Where the mountain climber died," Ryan murmured ominously.

From this vantage point, Sunny believed Ryan's old story. The rocky drop-off looked brutally desolate. A shiver passed through her. She was glad when they had sailed past.

"Oh—Windsong Place!" Delighted, Sunny gazed down at the familiar gables, verandas and turrets of the Victorian mansion. From here it looked like an elaborate dollhouse.

When the mansion had disappeared beyond their line of vision, it seemed the most natural thing in the world for Sunny to lean back against Ryan's wide, strong chest. His smoothly shaven chin rested against her temple; his warm, even breathing stirred her hair; dreamy contentment stole over her.

Ryan tugged at a cord every now and then, and sometimes with a roar and a *whoosh*, the basket would rise higher, catching an airstream that changed the direction of their flight.

"Is that how you steer it?"

Ryan nodded, happier than she had seen him in a long time. "It's a matter of raising and lowering the balloon to catch the air currents. Riding them."

With a pull of another cord, he lowered the balloon. Sunny looked up into the great cavernous interior of the brightly colored globe above them. A patch of azure sky had appeared in the balloon's fabric. She heard a gush of air surge out as they descended.

Ryan clicked on the walkie-talkie; in a few brief words, he described their current location. Which reminded Sunny that a crew in cars would be chasing them somewhere below.

She spotted a loose caravan of vehicles rounding the mountainous curves, headed in their direction. Wilbur's Jeep was among them. After a short while, the earth slowed its movement beneath them; treetops scraped against the bottom of their basket. They drifted down into a meadow, a smaller meadow than the first.

Ryan loosened his hold from her and she immediately missed his warmth, his nearness.

"It can't be over already," she whispered.

"It's not." His fingers beneath her chin, he tilted her face upward. His dark gray eyes were intense. He brushed his lips across hers—once, twice, lingered there, touching, tasting....

The kiss deepened and swept her away, higher than the balloon had taken her, far beyond the horizon. Giving her a breathtaking glimpse of eternity...

With a jolt and a harsh brushing sound, they put down in the meadow. Ryan drew away from her and Sunny became aware of the vehicles pulling to a halt around them.

"Take a bow," Ryan uttered softly. The old mocking coolness had returned.

Sunny caught sight of Lavinia and Wilbur, waving from their open-topped Jeep.

6

SATURDAY AFTERNOON, so far, had gone off without a hitch. Yet, it had been torture, Sunny reflected as she freshened her mauve lipstick at the oval mirror of the vanity table.

After the balloon ride, they had returned to Windsong Place and lunched with the Tanners in the backyard gazebo overlooking the river. The afternoon would have been pleasant enough, but Ryan's determination to present a picture of wedded bliss had begun to wear on her nerves.

He'd touched her freely—casual gestures involving her shoulders, her waist or the small of her back. More troubling was when he touched her mentally, with a private gaze that almost made her believe they *were* a couple.

Every possessive gesture or glance went straight through to her heart, because they *weren't* a couple. She was too vulnerable, and he was too damned good at pretending. She had to remind herself constantly that it was all a sham. And when it was over it would hurt too much if she let her guard down, even for a moment.

As she had on that balloon ride.

Pinning her hair up in a casual twist at the top of her head, Sunny glanced at the bedside clock. Almost four. Time for the next activity on her agenda: tea in the Oak Hall.

Mrs. Lee, the assistant innkeeper, had enthusiastically agreed to serve, and Malcolm the chef was preparing some of his favorite pastry recipes. Sunny hoped Lavinia would enjoy herself more than she had at the hot-air balloon activity. Ryan had gone off to inspect some part of the property. Sunny wondered if he'd return in time for tea.

She stepped into her soft springtime dress of periwinkle blue with a close-fitting bodice and gently flared skirt; the simple design was enriched by an off-the-shoulder ruffle.

As she zipped it up the back, she mentally reviewed the remaining items on her agenda for the day: Tea in the Oak Hall. Dinner in the inn's restaurant. Dancing to the music of a band she had hired to play in the ballroom. Then, bedtime.

The last item on the agenda set Sunny's stomach to churning. There was anxiety and also an odd, fatalistic sense of excitement.

The grandfather clock in the entrance hall chimed four as Sunny made her way down the stairway into the Oak Hall. Lavinia had invited the inn's guests, telling Sunny that the idea of high tea was "simply too marvelous to keep to ourselves."

Because the spring weather beckoned the younger guests outdoors, only a few of the older ones were gathered in front of the massive fireplace in the Oak Hall on that Saturday afternoon.

Lavinia was clothed in an expensive knit pantsuit, her dark hair was dressed in an elegant coiffure, and pearls glinted at her ears and throat. She fairly radiated culture as she sat in a wing chair before the fireplace, and Sunny felt like curtseying in her presence.

She introduced Sunny to the guests as "Mrs. Alexander."

"Please, call me Sunny." The introduction had unreasonably flustered her.

Lavinia whispered, "I forgot you use your maiden name. To be honest, I feel more comfortable introducing you as Mrs. Alexander. It's easier than explaining. Most of our guests are from the old school, you know."

Sunny decided she would set Lavinia straight on her use of her maiden name as soon as the purchase agreement was signed.

As the guests settled into armchairs, Sunny offered them their choice of tea, the individually wrapped tea bags handsomely showcased in a hand-carved walnut box. Mrs. Lee set freshly baked tea cakes, tarts and cookies on the tables between the wing chairs, then poured from a silver teapot into delicate cups of fine blue-patterned china.

Most guests seemed to be regulars, and Lavinia knew which interests had drawn them. With smooth expertise, she drew Sunny into the conversation with introductions such as, "Sunny, this is Sally Bowens. She's here for the Concerto-Aria Recital at Rosen Concert Hall. She's a musician. Didn't you perform there a few times, Sally?"

The thin elderly woman, who held her cup of Earl Grey tea with her pinky gracefully outstretched, went on to fondly reminisce of her performances in the nearby concert hall.

And, Lavinia continued, "Professor Collins stays with us every May. What is that flower you're researching, Professor?"

In his frumpy tan cardigan and baggy trousers, the professor rumbled with enthusiasm, "The Cullowhee lily." He removed the pipe from his mouth and bit into an apple tart. With his mouth full, he explained, "The Cherokees used its leaves for salad."

A short, wiry woman in jeans and a T-shirt declared, "I'm taking the grandkids fishing for hornybacks. Or trout, if our luck runs out."

As the guests conversed, munched and sipped, Sunny's eyes strayed frequently to the grandfather clock. Ryan hadn't returned. How could she want him here, yet dread his arrival?

The clock chimed five. "Tea has been a tremendous success," Lavinia pronounced as the guests dispersed. "I'll keep it as a daily function." The praise was gratifying.

A flock of other guests wandered in, most dressed elegantly for dinner. The side tables were set with cheese, crackers and wine.

Sunny was struggling to resist the impulse to go look for Ryan, when there was a lull in the conversation and all eyes turned to the tall, broad-shouldered newcomer in a taupe gabardine blazer who descended the staircase—serene and profoundly commanding, his gray eyes cool as he surveyed the small crowd.

Sunny's breath caught somewhere between her lungs and throat. *He is master here. He's come home.*

Lavinia introduced Ryan to the guests. Advancing at a leisurely pace, he responded with appropriate greetings. And then his gaze settled on Sunny. He halted in whatever he'd been saying. His gaze took in her dress, her hair. And as his stare lingered, a warmth rose within her. Her heartbeat pounded in her ears.

He's playing a part, she reminded herself. *Nothing more.* But it felt like more. And the night hadn't even begun yet.

AT DINNER, RYAN was subjected for the first time since his divorce to hearing Sunny introduced as *Mrs.* Alexander.

Each time he heard it, a small current of possessiveness pulsed through him. Mrs. Alexander. His wife. His.

He couldn't keep his eyes off her. Her violet-blue dress left her shapely shoulders bare and golden in the glow of candlelight. Her shiny, upswept hair allowed a few coy tendrils to curl against her throat, where pearls glistened, generating memories of when she'd worn *only* pearls. And he had made love to her, in front of the fireplace. On their honeymoon.

After a prime-rib supper in the dining room, they moved into the formal ballroom, where the three-man band Sunny had hired began their first set.

Lavinia had set up tables around the dance floor, which were now fully occupied. Wilbur had gone to talk to the guests, leaving Ryan and Sunny alone at the small, candle-lit table.

The band played soft, classic love songs.

"They're not bad," Ryan said, nodding toward the band, in an effort to start conversation with Sunny. He couldn't very well sit here all evening, staring at her. Not if he was going to take her to their room afterward and keep his hands off her.

"They're pretty good." She clutched a liqueur glass tightly and watched couples circle the dance floor.

So much for conversation. He tried again. "Thanks for your quick thinking when Wilbur brought up the tabloid article."

Sunny shrugged—a provocative movement of her shoulders that drew Ryan's attention to them again. He knew how soft and tender the curve of her neck would feel beneath his hands, beneath his mouth.

"I did what I had to do." She evaded his eyes. "You couldn't very well have denied being there on that yacht. Photographs don't lie."

Ryan's eyebrows rose. Could that be disapproval he heard in her voice? "Ah, yes. Me and Princess Catherine. Caught red-handed in a torrid love affair."

It wasn't true. He barely knew the woman. But he'd be damned if he'd admit that now. Not when he was almost sure Sunny's bottom lip had tightened at his remark and she was rising to his bait. "How did you know the details in that article?" he asked.

Her luminous green eyes met his, and the disapproval was clear. "Your grinning mug graced every grocery and convenience store for the entire month of February. And again in March. We're lucky the Tanners haven't found *that* article. Yet."

Her curt tone afforded Ryan a rush of illogical pleasure. He nodded gravely. "You must mean the one about me and the coffee heiress from Brazil." He rested his elbows on the table and leaned forward. "Funny, but I don't recall either one of those articles being on the front page of the tabloids. In fact, I thought they were both part of collages that featured people a lot more socially prominent than I."

Her cheeks colored delicately. "Maybe so. I can't remember that much about the articles. In fact, I probably wouldn't have noticed them at all if Fran, my assistant manager, hadn't brought them to my attention."

"Seems you spend a lot of time reading about me," he reflected aloud. "First business magazines, then tabloids..."

"Let's not forget rest-room walls."

He laughed. "God. Who do *they* have me with?"

Her eyes darkened with genuine disapproval that somehow pierced through his euphoria. "I'm glad you find your...your sexual notoriety...so amusing."

Before he could think better of it, he caught hold of her wrist. "Don't believe everything you read, Sunny. I didn't do anything more than talk to those women. And even if I had, it wouldn't have meant a thing."

Her pulse raced beneath his fingers. His own heartbeats shook him. He didn't have time to analyze what he had just admitted, or why it was true. Lavinia was seating herself beside him, with Wilbur on his other side.

Ryan released Sunny's wrist. Looked away from her stare.

"Why are you two sitting?" Lavinia set her drink down on the table. "Go ahead, Ryan. Dance with your wife."

Your wife. Again, hunger sliced through him. She *had* been his wife once. She had promised him forever.

The song was a slow one. Dancing would necessitate touching her. Holding her. And he wanted badly to do that.

"No, we're worn-out...." Sunny began to say, but Ryan stood and held his hand out to her.

"Let's go," he said. She owed him a dance. At least a dance.

She hesitated, but Lavinia was there, nagging her like a clucking hen until Sunny had no gracious choice. She ignored Ryan's hand—putting off the inevitable touching for as long as possible—but moved out onto the dance floor.

She cast him a hesitant glance over one bare shoulder. A few more blond tendrils had escaped from her French twist, trailing in wisps down the nape of her neck. Her violet-blue dress silhouetted intriguing curves beneath.

He couldn't wait any longer. With a hand at her elbow, he turned her and pulled her firmly against him. Looking somewhat flustered, she tried to give him her hand in a formal dance position, but he ignored it. Instead, he pulled her close and she was forced to loop her arms around his neck.

They moved stiffly at first, his face against her fragrant hair. She refused to relax. Refused to surrender to the familiar contours of their embrace.

But as the sensuous melody worked its magic, her body molded to his in the way it was meant to. Ryan's pleasure was so keen it almost hurt; she was softness, and warmth, and the very essence of womanhood. He closed his eyes.

Together they swayed and turned to the rhythm of the song. The music coaxed them further still into a subtle gyration of hips and shoulders. His body moved with hers. His blood heated. His breathing deepened. He swept his hand up her back, pressing her more tightly against him.

The fragrance of lilies in her hair and the softness of her skin sharpened his hunger. He imagined her without the silk dress, moving this way beneath him. An ache formed in his chest and radiated down through his midsection.

He wanted her so damn badly.

Without forethought, he pressed a kiss onto her tender, fragrant neck, just below her ear. He heard her inhale, and felt a slight tremble go through her. A responding heat flared up in him. It had been too damn long since he'd made her tremble in his arms.

He kissed her again, on the curve of her jaw, his need steadily growing. With a moan, she pulled back to gaze up at him, her eyes a dusky green, the pupils dilated in a way he well remembered. A way that made his arousal harden all the more.

"Ryan—" she breathed, uncertainty in her whisper.

"Shhh." He kissed her lips then. Softly at first, a mere brushing of his across hers. Her arms tightened around his neck. He coaxed her mouth opened, and then delved deeper. And deeper still. He hadn't forgotten her sweetness, not for a moment, in all the years he'd been without her.

The love song ended, replaced by a faster, intrusive beat, which reminded Ryan of where they were. Gruffly he whispered against her ear, "It's time to go upstairs."

Without waiting for a reply—he had all the response he needed in her upturned gaze—he hooked an arm around her slender waist and guided her with single-minded determination.

"But Wilbur and Lavinia," she objected.

Impatiently Ryan steered her toward their table, thanked them for the evening and bid them good-night.

Reeling from his sensual onslaught, Sunny did the same. Ryan then ushered her out of the ballroom and up the stairs. His face—dark, intense, exceedingly handsome—gave no clue to his thoughts, except for one: he wanted her.

And, God help her, she wanted him. Now, without thought. But as he extracted the room key from his pocket, rational thought *did* intrude upon her. If they made love, would he regret their involvement? Would it ruin the fragile friendship growing again between them? Sunny had to make sure Ryan knew exactly what he was doing, and not acting on impulse, or tomorrow he would turn from her with bitter self-recriminations.

She clutched his arm as they reached their room, feeling his hard muscles beneath the gabardine of his blazer. "Ryan, wait."

He gazed down at her with smoky gray eyes. Then he kissed her again, there in the corridor outside their room, with a slow fierceness that sent her blood rushing hotly through her veins.

She wanted him. Tonight. His hands swept up the curve of her waist and captured her breasts beneath the silken ruffle. His thumbs roused her to hardness as he continued to kiss her.

He stopped only to shove the room key into the lock.

"Ryan," she gasped, "you *do* realize what you're doing, don't you? This isn't part of our deal...."

As she waited for him to assure her it wasn't, and that he wouldn't regret their involvement later, the passionate need in his eyes suddenly cooled. Like a fire doused with ice water.

"Then by all means," he replied, "let's not work overtime." He withdrew his hands and strode down the corridor.

SUNDAY MORNING, Ryan woke to a loud knock on the door and an excited maid calling, "Mrs. Alexander! Come quick. The horses are here!"

Sunny, who had obviously been up for a while, came flying out of the dressing room, buttoning her blouse as she hurried toward the door. "Horses? Did you say horses? What horses?"

Before Ryan could mutter an explanation, Sunny had bounded out the door, her blond curls an unruly mop, her golden brows drawn together in perplexity.

Ryan fell back down onto the narrow fold-up cot he had purchased at the army-navy store in Heaven's Hollow yesterday and smuggled to the room under the cover of darkness. He wondered if he had slept at all. He really wasn't sure. When he had returned to the bedroom after his long nocturnal march through the woods— imperative to let his frustration cool—Sunny had been fast asleep in bed, the covers drawn up to her chin.

It had taken him hours to grapple with his anger, then harness it and convert it to a useful emotion. Like gratitude. Yes, gratitude. He was grateful to Sunny. Grateful.

She had saved them both a great deal of embarrassment. This hormonal thing between them had simply overpowered his good judgment. He shouldn't have kissed her. She'd been right to stop him, he told himself as he showered and shaved and replayed every nuance of the evening in his mind. As he zipped up his jeans, he heard the bedroom door open.

Sunny called out, "Ryan?"

He shrugged into a denim shirt as Sunny rounded the corner and stopped short at the sight of him. Her cheeks were flushed, her green eyes sparkled with excitement and her full lips were parted as if she wanted to say something.

He turned to reach for his leather belt, and she whispered, "Thanks, Ry. For the horses. I never expected..." She broke off and turned away from him.

TO SUNNY'S DELIGHT, the horses had arrived just in time for the picnic she had planned for the day. Malcolm had prepared an exquisite lunch to Sunny's specifications: a carafe of sparkling cider, a loaf of home-baked bread, a wheel of Brie, fresh fruit and chicken salad, all nestled in a wicker basket.

Even the weather cooperated—she couldn't have asked for a fairer, brighter day. The only snag in her plans was Lavinia.

"Sunny, I'm worn-out from yesterday. Have Malcolm divide the lunch into two baskets. You and Ryan can go off on your own. Wilbur and I will take ours to the garden gazebo."

"But Lavinia, we have horses now! We can ride the trails, and stop to picnic beside a brook."

"Horses! My word! I haven't ridden a horse in thirty years. No, no, dear, you and Ryan enjoy the day. It's a wonderful plan—the guests would adore it, I'm sure—but Wilbur and I will feast in the backyard gazebo."

No amount of persuasion would change Lavinia's mind, but Sunny wasn't about to let Ryan's extravagant gesture of having horses shipped in for the week go to waste. By ten that morning, Ryan and she headed out down a shady trail into the mountain forest of Windsong Place, the wicker picnic basket firmly secured to her horse, and a blanket secured to Ryan's.

She had known he wouldn't refuse, no matter how dark his mood was. Ryan loved horses, and he loved riding through the woods. So did she.

In companionable silence, they enjoyed traversing the trails, crossing mountain streams and galloping across open meadows. When the sun had risen high in the blazing blue sky, they reined in their horses beside a cool, gurgling brook, and shared the picnic lunch.

It should have been an idyllic meal. Perhaps even romantic. But Ryan had taken his plate to a large, flat boulder beside the stream, leaving Sunny to eat alone on the blanket. Not a word was exchanged between them.

Sunny wondered what had caused his black mood. If anyone had a right to be angry, it was she. He had kissed her into a swelter of need last night, then left her high and dry at the bedroom door. She clenched her jaw as she remembered his flippant words: *let's not work overtime.* She wouldn't lose her head with him again, she swore it. He wanted a professional relationship, and that's just what he'd get.

Ryan, meanwhile, wondered why in the hell Sunny was clenching her jaw. Was she nursing a grudge because he'd kissed her last night? From the boulder where he sat, he picked up a flat stone and skipped it across the natural, sunlit pool. They had once called this their swimming hole. They had laughed and played here as children. Years later, they'd skinny-dipped. And made love.

Ryan tightened his fist, and another small stone he'd been about to throw crumpled to pieces in his closed palm. Gratitude—that's what he should feel toward her. For reminding him of the purpose behind their kisses last night. He tossed the crumpled rock into the water.

"Want more sparkling cider?" she called from the blanket.

"No." Against his better judgment, Ryan snuck another glance at her. She was wearing tight white jeans and a blouse of nearly translucent floral print with sleeves that billowed down to her elbows. She looked clean, fresh and young, and the noonday sunshine was turning her hair from platinum to gold, so it looked like a dazzling halo.

He averted his face. It was easier to feel grateful when he wasn't looking at her. "I think we should head back."

As he stood up, a family trooped down the path—a cheery red-haired couple with half a dozen chattering, giggling children. The adults sat on a granite boulder, while the kids ran, leaped and cavorted in all directions— toward the stream, the woods and the horses.

Ryan saw Sunny gazing at the frolicking children with a wistful expression. He'd seen that look in her eyes before, and every time it packed a surprising punch to his gut.

She was thinking about their baby. Their lost baby.

He towered above her as she watched two carrot-topped boys skipping across the brook on rocks. Her eyes, fixed on the children, were suspiciously bright. "Sunny?"

"Hmmm?"

Ryan dropped down onto the blanket beside her. She was so lovely, so incredibly lovely. He wanted to take the pain away from her. A pain she wouldn't have had to live with if he hadn't deliberately seduced her—overcome her reluctance with determined kisses and the most potent wine he could find—that summer so long ago. She had just turned eighteen. *Eighteen.* And though he'd been a mere twenty—a week shy of twenty-one—he still felt responsible.

He tried to assuage his guilt by telling himself that if he hadn't taken her virginity, someone else would have. But in his heart, he didn't believe it. She wouldn't have given in to anyone else. Not then. Perhaps not for years, when she would have been more worldly.

"Aren't they cute, Ry?" she asked softly, nodding toward the boys.

"I suppose so." He felt helpless against her anguish; against his own guilt. "Maybe I *will* have some more of that cider." He took the half-empty carafe out of the picnic basket that Sunny had just repacked, along with two wineglasses.

"Ours would have been about the age of that one," ruminated Sunny. "The boy jumping across the rock. Or maybe smaller, like the one climbing that tree. I'd say they're both around nine or ten, wouldn't you?"

"Here." Ryan handed her a glass of sparkling cider, wrapped her hand around the glass and kept his hand over hers for a moment. She glanced at him in surprise. He didn't know what to say. He searched for words that might soothe her, but he couldn't find any. Never could.

She seemed to know his intent, anyway. "I'm okay." She smiled lopsidedly and took the glass. "I've been fine for years. I even teach art classes to kids in the summer. I don't know why I've been so melancholy in the last few days about children. It must be this place. Or maybe being with you again." Her voice caught, and she looked quickly away from him. "We would have been parents, you and I."

The idea of having a child with Sunny lodged like a bullet in Ryan's chest. He had wanted their son or daughter, maybe even more than she had.

An irreverent thought occurred to him. A child would have tied Sunny to him. Permanently.

"Maybe things have worked out for the best," he mused. "I might not have made a very good father. I don't know much about kids. I've never been around them." The chaos of conflicting emotions made his words harsher than he intended. "I probably won't be in the future, either."

"You don't want a family?" She sounded incredulous.

"Not especially." After he said it, he could have kicked himself. Her eyes had darkened again with that same pain—the one that had overwhelmed her at their baby's death; the one that had driven her away from him.

"Then I guess things *have* worked out for the best," she said in a choked whisper.

"Sunny, you know damned well I wasn't talking about... about us, or our baby. I would have wanted...I mean, I *did* want . . . oh, hell. You know what I mean." Every word seemed to alienate her more, and his confusion deepened. To change the subject, he asked morosely, "What about you? Do you plan to have children?"

"Definitely."

His gaze settled on her. He wasn't sure why he was surprised; she'd always wanted children. Or more precisely, a family. As a child, she'd been planted into one stepfamily after another, just long enough for her love to take root, only to be plucked out again by her flighty mother after another divorce. The only permanence Sunny had found was with her grandmother, Olive, during summers, here at Windsong Place.

Which had ended with *their* divorce.

"Definitely?" Ryan repeated. He took a gulp of sweet, cold cider, swooshed it around in his mouth and wondered just how definite her child-bearing plans were. Surely she wasn't—?

"When I'm married, of course," she specified. Ryan choked on the cider, managed to swallow it and coughed. She hit him on the back in concern. "Are you okay?"

He nodded, and when he had regained his breath, croaked out, "Married? You're getting married?"

"Not any time soon. First I want to be established in my career. But if this purchase goes through, I should be well on my way to achieving that."

Ryan felt stunned. Shell-shocked. "Who's the lucky guy?"

She averted her eyes again, looking embarrassed. "I didn't mean that I'm engaged. I'm talking about future plans."

"But you must have someone in mind."

She took a sip of the cider. "In a way."

"In a way? What's that supposed to mean?"

"I mean, I have an idea of what my Mr. Right will be like."

A strong, dizzying relief filled Ryan. She hadn't yet found her "Mr. Right." Silently he cursed her mother for her several marriages and divorces. No wonder Sunny craved permanence. But in Ryan's opinion, marriage was certainly no way to find it. Nothing, absolutely nothing, could guarantee "forever." Not even a wedding vow, as he knew from experience.

She continued in a stronger voice, "Practicality is the key. I'll find a man with the qualities I want in a husband. And I'll make sure that this time, the marriage lasts."

Ryan's mouth tightened. Unlike their marriage, she meant.

"You're saying you're going to hunt for Mr. Right with some kind of a shopping list?" he asked derisively.

"Not *hunt*. But I will keep my mind open to possibilities."

"Let's hear this list of, uh, qualities," Ryan urged, interested in spite of the heaviness that had settled over him.

She hesitated a moment. "To begin with, I'd like him to have philosophies in keeping with mine. For example, you know I feel very strongly about the fate of fur-bearing animals. Fox, mink, beaver. I'd never marry a man who bought fur products."

Ryan almost laughed out loud, but managed to control his mirth. "I have heard that mink-murderers make lousy husbands."

She directed a sharp side-glance at him. "You don't think similar ideals are important?"

"Of course I do. Really. Go on. Tell me more."

"He'd have to have a sense of humor."

Ryan nodded in total agreement. "Essential for the sake of anyone involved with you."

Sunny acknowledged his mockery with a droll smirk, but otherwise ignored it. "He has to be successful in his career, or at least a hard worker, since he'll be my lifelong partner."

"Now, that's sensible. Will you require a résumé?"

"Hopefully his life-style will reflect his efforts."

"Rich, you mean."

"Not necessarily," she protested, disturbed by the implication. "Just industrious. *And* he must sincerely like children. That's very important."

"This guy has my heartfelt admiration already."

"It would be nice if he were reasonably attractive, too. Not necessarily knock-'em-dead handsome like you."

Ryan cast her a sardonic glance, expecting to find a teasing light in her eyes. But there was no levity in her straight-ahead gaze. Only contemplation. He finished his cider and curtly pushed the empty glass down into the picnic basket.

If her Mr. Right ever hurt her, he'd kill the bastard.

To lighten his darkening mood, Ryan muttered, "So he has to have money, humor, patience, looks and no opinion contrary to yours."

His sarcastic tone was lost on her. She nodded with perfect seriousness. "Yes, and one more thing."

Ryan lifted his brows, waiting for her to go on.

Sunny fidgeted with a wild daisy she had plucked from the grass. Ryan shifted uncomfortably on the blanket beside her. Her blush spoke vividly of her last requirement, whether she realized it or not.

Some invisible python wrapped around his chest and squeezed. He didn't want to envision her making love to some other man. *Refused to do so*.

Sunny evaded the last qualification on her list with a bright and breezy "Anyway, what do you think?"

Ryan scowled. "I think you're crazy." As much as he tried to fight it, his earlier resentment had returned, stronger than ever. And a question formed itself in his gut: *Which ones of those qualities had he been lacking? Why had she left him?*

But he knew the answer. They'd discussed it at the time. She'd left him because there'd been no reason to stay. Neither of them had particularly wanted to marry. They'd done so for the sake of the baby. And when the baby had died, so had their marriage. Simple, straightforward, logical.

"Marriage is emotional suicide," muttered Ryan. "It encourages both parties to become too dependent on the other. It fosters a dangerous illusion."

"You mean, the illusion of . . . love?" she asked quietly.

The word deepened his illogical anger. He refused even to repeat it. "Or something equally destructive. Show me a miserable human being, and I'll show you a victim of...emotional dependence." He snatched the empty glass from her fingers, stuffed it into the basket and stood up.

He had to get out of here. Away from her. Away from the chaos roiling inside him.

Rock climbing. That's what he needed. Something strenuous and challenging enough to wear himself out, both mentally and physically. "I think you should head back to the inn. Take the blanket and basket with you."

Sunny stood up, but made no move toward either the blanket or the basket. The couple with the children had moved on, their happy voices fading into silence. Ryan and she were alone.

"Where are you going?" she asked.

He nodded toward one of the huge, hulking peaks beyond the hemlock forest. "I'm going to ride up to Devil's Ridge."

"Devil's Ridge?" To his amazement, her face actually paled. "Last night I dreamed about you on Devil's Ridge."

"Dreamed . . . ?" He quirked his mouth up mockingly. "I'm flattered that you've been dreaming about me, but I'm not sure if it's politically correct in regards to your, uh, employer." Last night's anger merged with today's, and he emphasized the last word.

"The dream was so clear, it woke me up. Ryan, *you fell.*"

He stared at her. She looked scared. Her sudden emotional intensity surprised and intrigued him. Lessened some of the heaviness inside him. "Sunny, none of your 'prophetic dreams' have ever come true before."

"So what? You know men have died falling from that rock. Why would you want to chance it?"

"Maybe heights just turn me on."

"Maybe risking your neck turns you on."

He lifted a shoulder in a negligent shrug. "Maybe."

"I know about all those crazy stunts you've pulled. Skydiving, hang gliding, bungee-jumping." She was pale, and her lips trembled. Like potent wine, her worry warmed his chest.

"More tabloid gossip," he murmured. "I've never bungee-jumped. Thought about it, but—"

"Ryan, I'm serious. I won't let you go up there."

"You won't *let* me?" he said in a disbelieving tone.

"That's right." She squared her jaw, ready to fight.

Amused at her stance, at her obstinacy, he softly taunted, "You gonna fight me, Short Stuff?" He wasn't sure where the old nickname came from. He hadn't thought of it in twenty years.

"Yes, I *will* fight you," she vowed. "Any way I can."

"Should be interesting." Visions of wrestling with her swam before his eyes. Of forcing her down onto the blanket. Pinning her beneath him. Unbuttoning her blouse, kissing her resistance away. He felt his body respond to the prospect, his hunger returning full force.

Ten years, he thought with self-loathing, hadn't helped him at all. Sunny still meant trouble. Big trouble. Instantaneous combustion every time he touched her. Or even *thought* about it.

Furious with himself, and with her, he muttered, "Okay. I won't ride up to Devil's Ridge." She gaped at him, clearly surprise by her victory. "But I am going to ride the trails. Alone."

Silently, he added, *Until I'm so damned tired I can't even think about touching you.*

AS RYAN SET OFF on horseback through the dense mountain forest, Sunny left the blanket and picnic basket at the base of the giant oak and obstinately guided her mount behind him. He ignored her completely, which was fine with her.

She had only one reason for accompanying him on this ride —her dream from last night. A sense of foreboding filled her as she remembered waking in the middle of the night crying out his name. *Ryan had fallen from Devil's Ridge.*

Though none of her dreams had come true before, she hated to think this one might. Even if she *had* felt like plotting his murder last night, after he'd left her alone.

She tightened her hold on the reins. His desire had been real on that dance floor, and later, too, upstairs. That wasn't part of his performance, as he wanted her to believe. But then, desire had never been lacking between them—not since they'd broached adulthood. In fact, desire had been their downfall as friends. Perhaps that was why he was so determined to keep their relationship "professional."

She was grateful, actually, that he had come to his senses when he had. Yes, she decided, she was grateful. Because God knew she wouldn't have come around, and without a doubt, she would have regretted the lapse later.

With a frustrated sigh, she urged her horse up a steep incline, trying her best to keep pace with Ryan. After a good hour or so of riding up twisting paths, across muddy ravines and through dense forests, they finally came to a wide, well-traveled path where they stopped to rest their horses. From the way her ears felt, Sunny knew they'd reached a relatively high elevation.

Suddenly, a loud, piercing wail—a woman's scream—broke the stillness and jarred the tethered horses into restlessness.

With a glance at each other, Ryan and Sunny climbed an embankment toward the sound. It was only when they reached the top that Sunny recognized where they were. Her heart stopped.

They stood on Devil's Ridge.

7

BESIDE A STEEL FENCE lined with danger signs, a stout woman in a navy-blue wind suit stood on a huge granite boulder, her round, unadorned face white with panic. "Jonathon went over the cliff!" she cried. "He climbed this rock to get over the fence. I told him to get down, but he wouldn't listen."

Beyond the fence lay a sheer drop onto a rocky gorge. Dread clutched Sunny's heart.

"Stay here," Ryan told her. He followed Jonathon's route up the boulder, across the fence and down onto the rocky gray ledge. "He's okay," Ryan called. "He's on another ledge."

Sunny held her hands to her heart in relief. But it was a shaky, tentative relief. Jonathon, whoever he was, was still stranded on Devil's Ridge, a mile above a rocky gorge.

"The kid took off the minute my back was turned," whined the woman. "He outran me."

"Are you his mother?" Sunny felt certain she wasn't.

"His nanny. Should've given my notice weeks ago. I don't get paid enough to chase him up mountains."

Sunny cast her a blistering stare. "Will you go for help, or shall I?"

"I will. I'd rather not see—" The woman broke off mid-sentence, looking somewhat ashamed of herself, and hurried in the opposite direction from Windsong Place.

"Hey!" called Sunny. "Windsong Place is *that* way."

"Yeah, well we live *that* way." She pointed westward.

"Take my horse. It's tied up down there."

"No, thanks. I'd rather walk." The woman disappeared down the westward, twisting path. Sunny prayed it wouldn't take her long to get to a phone.

Weaving her fingers through the steel mesh fence, Sunny watched Ryan stretch out on his stomach at the edge of the precipice, his black hair whipping around his somber face. Fear drummed in her ears. *He was too close to the edge.*

Her dream replayed itself vividly in her mind. Ryan edging along Devil's Ridge. A sudden shout, a dislodging of rock. Him plunging into the rocky gorge below...

"Ryan," she cried, aching with fear. "Come back here. I'll get the boy."

"Don't be crazy. You'd never be able to pull him up. Stay behind the fence, Sunny." Then he called down to the child, "You okay, Jonathon?"

"A little dizzy is all" came the faint reply in a boyish voice.

Sunny climbed up the boulder and found a smooth place to get a grip on the sharp-topped steel fence. When she found one, she supported her weight on her hands, then carefully swung one leg over, looking for a good toehold in the steel mesh. As she straddled the fence, she resisted the suicidal urge to turn around and peer over the edge of the cliff.

"Listen to me carefully, Jonathon," ordered Ryan. "Don't look down, understand? Just look up here at me. That's good. Now, I'm going to help you climb up."

"I'm not ready to come up yet."

Sunny couldn't believe her ears. How could any human being stand at the edge of death without panicking? But the boy sounded calm enough. His stoic attitude helped to ease the panic that threatened to overcome her as she lowered herself from the fence to the forbidden side.

If a child could keep his head while clinging to the side of a vertical cliff, couldn't she keep hers, standing on solid ground?

Despite her resolve to stay calm, her heart rose to her throat as she peeked over the ledge. She could see no bottom. Only a jagged rocky wall on the other side of the gorge, and vast, gray nothingness below.

Dizziness rushed over her. Her pulse thudded and her mouth went dry. What if the land should give way? *If Ryan were to die, how could I bear to live?* The thought shook her to the core, locked her into immobility.

Silently, devoutly, she prayed. Dropping to her knees, she edged her way closer to the cliff. She had to be there if Ryan needed her. Holding her breath, she narrowed her vision to include only the child who knelt on a lower ledge and not the sheer drop beneath him.

Kneeling on a narrow ledge with his small hands gripping a root that jutted out from the gray-and-russet rock wall, was a boy who looked no older than eight. His straight auburn hair was cut like an upside-down bowl and matched his amber eyes. A spray of freckles dusted his nose.

An odd, numbing calm stole over Sunny. They had to bring him up to safety. She'd think no further than that.

"Give me your hand," commanded Ryan, reaching for him.

The boy squinted up at them, and Sunny was surprised to see defiance in his pale, oval face. "No," he said, "I have to get that flower." He glanced at a solitary white bloom that grew a few feet out of his reach. "It's a Cullowhee Lily, like the one in Professor Collins's book. He says they're very rare." Fervently, he added, "My pa will be proud I found it."

"Tell you what, kid," Ryan said in a conversational tone. "If you give me your hand, I'll get the flower for you."

"No." A shower of dirt and rocks sprayed downward beneath his high-topped sneaker as the boy moved a step farther away. His hands clutched convulsively at the rock-bound tree root.

Sunny swallowed a hysterical sob that was bubbling up in her. Another false move, if the boy dislodged the wrong rock, both he and Ryan could plunge to their deaths. Fear returned to her in a sickening blast.

Jonathon peered up at them, his face now chalky white with fear of his own. Still, obstinate determination burned in his amber eyes. "You might be tricking me. You might not get the lily. And I *need* it." His desperation seemed incongruous, until he said, "My pa might not believe I found it."

Ryan looked at Sunny with a mute call for help.

Through a constricted throat, she managed to say steadily enough, "If you come with us, Jonathon, we'll bring your father up here to see the lily. We'd tell him how you found it."

Jonathon shook his head, scaring her with his movement. "He won't have time to come up here. He's real busy."

She tried to think of a persuasive response, but panic clouded her mind.

"If you pick the lily, it'll die," Ryan stated firmly. "What good is a dead flower?" Only by the twitching of a muscle in his jaw could Sunny detect his tension.

"Cullowhee lilies are almost stinked. Professor Collins said so. That means they're real, real special."

"So are Pluto Power Crystals," replied Ryan.

Sunny and the boy both frowned at him. Jonathon asked, "What kind of crystals?"

"Pluto Power Crystals. Taken from a meteor that fell from Pluto. You have heard of the planet Pluto, haven't you?" Ryan spoke with such authority, Sunny almost believed him.

Jonathon closed one eye against the sun, tilted his head and nodded.

Ryan rolled to the side and dug into his pocket, coming out with a small purple stone that he held up for the boy to see. "Here it is. This is a lot rarer than any kind of lily." The smooth chunk of amethyst glinted purple in the sunlight. Sunny recognized the gem. It was Ryan's good luck charm—a small piece of amethyst his father had brought him back from his travels; Ryan had been about Jonathon's age at the time.

He'd kept it all these years! On his person, it seemed. Sunny found it easier to believe the stone came from Pluto.

"And it's magic," Ryan added. "You can have it if you come up here now."

Staring at the stone, Jonathon wrinkled his freckled nose. "Is it really magic, or are you trying to fool me?"

Ryan shrugged. "It always worked for me." Softly, he added, "You could wish for your pa to come see your lily."

Jonathon stared up at him doubtfully. An indecisive moment ticked by. His mouth twisted with regret. "I can't take your Pluto Power Crystal," he murmured, "because you're a stranger. I'm not allowed to take things from strangers." He chanced another glance toward the flower on the distant ledge. "But I better not pick that lily, either." Glumly, he explained, "If it's almost stinked, it shouldn't die."

Ryan stared at the boy. Sunny saw surprise in his gray eyes. And respect. The kind one man gives another when he's earned it.

The child saw it, too. His amber eyes grew bright, his thin shoulders squared. Like a flower in sunlight, he blossomed. "Yeah, I'll let the Cullowhee lily grow."

Ryan nodded and held out his hand.

Cautiously, Jonathon rose to his feet. Sunny sucked in her breath and prayed. Jonathon reached upward. Ryan's large hand closed around his small one. Slowly, cautiously, he pulled Jonathon up. The boy's jeans and sneakers scraped against stones, dislodging a small avalanche below.

Sunny's heartbeats shook her.

Shifting to his knees for more leverage, Ryan gave a final heave and fell backward, the boy tucked against his chest like a football in a quarterback's arms during a violent tackle.

He expelled a hard breath, then another. He turned Jonathon by his shoulders and stared at him sternly. "Never climb that fence. You might have fallen. And died. There's only one of *you* in this world, too. That makes you almost extinct."

Surprise now shone in Jonathon's eyes. "It does? Wow!" Clearly impressed, he vowed, "I won't climb the fence again. Ever. I promise."

Their gazes held—man's and boy's. Ryan nodded, accepting his word. "You made the right choice back there, son."

Jonathon's thin chest expanded beneath his gray sweatshirt. He put his arms around Ryan's neck and hugged him. For a reason Sunny couldn't quite fathom, she felt like crying.

After a thorough mussing of Jonathon's auburn mop, Ryan helped Sunny climb the fence, then boosted the boy over; he scampered down the boulder on the other side.

When Ryan had hoisted himself over the fence, a husky, uniformed sheriff's deputy came huffing toward them.

"The boy okay?" he called.

Ryan nodded. The deputy asked a few more questions, then some of Jonathon. Ryan drew the officer to the side and handed him the amethyst stone—the Pluto Power Crystal. With a brief smile, the deputy ushered Jonathon back down the path that led to his house.

Ryan stood staring in the direction they had taken, his hands curled at his sides. Silently, Sunny tucked her hand into the crook of his arm. He turned abruptly and pulled her into a hug, pressing his wind-cooled cheek against hers. He held her so tightly she could barely breathe. They clung together in silence, the aftershock of near disaster freezing them with visions of what might have been.

"He almost fell, Sunny," Ryan said. "To his death. Reaching for a flower to—" he drew in a steadying breath "—to make his father proud."

She heard the tremor in his whisper and a deep, warm emotion welled up inside of her. "But you were there for him."

There for him. The words echoed deep within Ryan's heart, touching places too painful to examine. She hadn't been referring to his physical presence on that ledge.

The hushed rustling of the mountain forest took on the solemnity of a thankful prayer. A wistful prayer.

When her throat had loosened enough, Sunny said, "A kid like that—" She gave a soft little laugh. "Well, someday he *will* make his father proud."

Ryan, too, gave a little laugh, but it was harsh, devoid of humor. It chilled Sunny to hear it, because she remembered the little boy he had been, once upon a time, with eyes as needful as Jonathon's.

After a while, Sunny felt Ryan relax his embrace. "Your prophecy didn't come true, Short Stuff." His tone was light, but the look in his silvery eyes was oddly poignant. "I didn't fall off Devil's Ridge."

"Not this time, at least. Thank God."

Ryan glanced back at the Ridge. Then down at Sunny. "There won't be a next time."

It was a promise Ryan knew he'd keep. For when he had peered down that rocky cliff into the gorge miles below, he had experienced no thrill. Not even a ghost of one. Only a strong, inner warning of peril. And a sharp regret at the thought of dying. He had too many things left unresolved.

Like Sunny. He hadn't yet made love to her. Hadn't reclaimed her as his own.

But now, as Ryan basked in her approving gaze, the inner warning sounded again. Here also lies danger. And he forced those near-death revelations from his mind.

THEY RODE THEIR HORSES back to the inn, stopping only to gather the picnic basket and blanket from beneath the towering oak tree. By the time they arrived at Windsong Place, a small crowd of guests had gathered on the front porch.

Someone shouted, "Here they come now."

The crowd parted, and Lavinia glided down the front steps, past the pink azalea garden. She smiled warmly as they dismounted and handed their reins to the gardener.

"I'm so proud of you two, I could just burst." Lavinia extended her arms to include both Ryan and Sunny in her hug. "We're so fortunate you were here." Stepping between them, she placed a hand on each of their backs and guided them up the garden stairs. "Come, tell us about the rescue. We're dying to hear."

"How in the world did you hear about it?" asked Sunny.

"A reporter from the local newspaper called. I swear they have the sheriff's office bugged. He's on his way over to interview you."

"Interview us?" Ryan repeated incredulously. "For what? We gave a kid a helping hand, that's all."

"Spoken like a true hero," Lavinia gushed as they reached the front porch. "But the reporter's going to want details. Like exactly where the Barrett boy was stranded, how you managed to pull him to safety—"

"Barrett boy? His name's Barrett?"

"Yes. Son of the country-western star. I suppose that had a lot to do with the media's quick response.

Ryan's brows furrowed. "He's Grady Barrett's son?"

"Why, yes, he is," confirmed Lavinia. "Jonathon lives in the house next door. With his father." She paused, then added, "Actually, with that sour-faced nanny of his. Jonathon sneaks over here to visit us whenever he can. Grady spends most of his time on the road, performing."

Ryan couldn't picture Grady, his boyhood pal from the house next door, as a father. Obviously, neither could Grady.

"Where's Jonathon's mother?" asked Sunny, more concerned about the boy than with his father's identity.

"Paris, maybe?" Lavinia shrugged. "Timbuktu? She and Grady are divorced. Anyway, we don't have much time to chat. The reporter should be coming soon. Oh, there's the news van now."

The interview lasted only moments, during which a young, bespectacled reporter recorded Ryan's and Sunny's responses. Ryan cut the interview short by professing to be hungry and tired, for which Sunny was grateful; she herself wanted nothing more than a hot bath, a good meal and a rest.

After the reporter left, Lavinia shooed the guests into the Oak Hall for tea, handed Sunny a menu and told the chef to send whatever dishes Mrs. Alexander ordered to their room. "Sunday nights are quiet. I figured you'd enjoy privacy this evening."

Ryan hesitated at the foot of the Grand Stairway. Privacy. That was the last thing he and Sunny needed. "Where's Wilbur? I have a few questions to ask him about renovations."

Lavinia colored slightly. "To be perfectly honest, he's driven into Asheville to meet with the other bidder. Just to let him down gently, you understand. The poor man wanted to buy Windsong Place in the worst way. Wilbur agreed to have dinner with him in town. But don't let it worry you."

As Ryan and Sunny ascended the stairway, they shared a glance loaded with doubts. They both knew Ryan's father a little too well to not worry.

AFTER A HOT, RELAXING shower, Ryan dressed in soft faded jeans and an old college sweatshirt, then stepped out onto the veranda of their private suite, into the softness of the May evening. Sunny sat beside the small round table, where fragrant dishes steamed; she was staring at the mountains silhouetted in the deep gold of twilight.

Ryan pulled out a chair, and Sunny's luminous green eyes took on a welcoming warmth. "Shrimp and pork egg rolls. Sizzling rice soup. Chinese vegetables. Szechuan chicken."

All his favorite dishes. He sat down with his uneasiness growing. Ten years they had been apart, and she remembered his favorite meal. Why did he find that fact so disturbing? So . . . provocative?

Before he could help himself, Sunny dished him out a good-sized portion of everything. She even mixed the duck sauce with just the right amount of hot mustard on a side dish for him to dip his egg roll.

"A meal fit for a hero," she quipped.

At last. Something he could gripe about. "Don't you start that hero stuff now. I've had about all I can take of that. What the hell would anyone else have done? Twiddle their thumbs and watch the kid fall?"

Her full, shapely lips curved into a grin. "Face it—you were magnificent."

Ryan scowled and ate in obstinate silence.

Sunny didn't say much, either. When she had finished only a bowl of sizzling rice soup, she set down her Oriental spoon and strolled over to the railing to gaze up at the sky. It had darkened to a rich butterscotch streaked with magenta.

Ryan couldn't help but watch the leisurely sway of her hips as she moved. The warm breeze ruffled her silky curls.

He realized then his plan had backfired. The extensive physical exertion of the day had *not* lessened his dangerous longing for her. He wanted her even more now, with an even deeper hunger.

He forced his attention away from Sunny and concentrated on his Szechuan chicken.

Sunny attributed his silence to exhaustion. She knew he hadn't slept much the past two nights. After today's hike, he probably needed a good, long sleep.

"You take the bed tonight," she said. "I'll take the cot."

"The cot is mine." He didn't raise his eyes from his plate.

Sunny decided he didn't look or act sleepy at all. He looked . . . explosive. A shiver raced through her. *Rescue me now,* she thought. *Reach out your hand. Pull me to you.*

Biting the corner of her lip, Sunny turned her eyes toward the mountains. This stark longing for Ryan had somehow worn her defenses thin. No doubt because of the intensely emotional day.

She had almost lost him. Irrevocably. Not as a lover—she had lost him that way years ago. But in those fearful moments on Devil's Ridge, she had realized with astounding clarity how vital it was that Ryan Alexander share the same planet with her. The same time span etched out of eternity. She had promised God anything—everything—if only He'd keep Ryan safe.

Sunny filled her lungs deeply with the fragrant air, as if she'd been drowning.

Not only had he survived, but he had saved a child's life. And established a bond with him in a way she could not have. In doing so, he had shown a side of himself he always tried so hard to hide—his compassion, his sensitivity.

Sunny's hands trembled on the veranda railing. Ryan had turned to *her* after he'd mastered the crisis. He had hugged her, struggled with tears. She'd wanted to go on holding him. She'd wanted to kiss him...make love to him until their passion melted away the sadness that loomed just beyond her reach.

The longing in her intensified.

Her prayers had been answered today. She'd said she'd be satisfied sharing a planet with him. But thinking of her desperate prayers only reminded her of how vulnerable human beings were, how short a person's life could be.

He could die tomorrow. Without ever making love to her again. The realization stunned her. Left her feeling bereft. She couldn't let that happen.

"Think I'll go take my bath now," she whispered. He didn't look up from his meal as she quickly made her way past him.

SOMETIME DURING HER flower-scented bath, the truth came to Sunny quite clearly. Its simplicity almost made her laugh. Why was she trying so hard to resist her physical longing for Ryan?

They were both mature, independent, secure adults now, not impressionable youths. Neither of them would "get into trouble," as her grandmother had so often phrased it. And no matter how often Ryan might remind her that she was his employee, she knew in her heart she was more than that.

She was an integral part of his past. They had grown up together. Courted. Married—even if it had been a humiliatingly short, painful marriage. They certainly wouldn't make *that* mistake again.

So why couldn't they behave like any two normal, single adults who were physically attracted to each other, and happened to be sharing the same bedroom?

When she thought of it in that light, she realized exactly what their problem had been lately—they weren't being *honest* with each other. At least, she wasn't being honest with him. By hiding her desire for him, wasn't she, in effect, lying?

Truth. That's what was lacking between them. Yes, indeed. The truth would set her free. She hoped.

In a zippered pocket within her purse, she found a condom tucked away long ago, just in case she'd ever needed it. She would need it tonight.

She brushed her hair to a radiant glow, glossed her lips to a pearly shimmer, and slipped into a long, diaphanous ivory gown that floated around her as she walked. The temptation was strong to add its matching robe, which would have kept the ensemble modest, the way she originally had intended to wear it. But she resisted the impulse. With her heart tripping over itself, she left the robe draped across the vanity chair.

With her fingers wrapped tightly around the condom, she stepped out of the tiny dressing room wearing only the translucent gown.

A small bedside lamp cast golden shadows as she slowly glided across the suite. Her nervousness increased with each step. The room was silent. Where was he?

She found him lying on the narrow cot, with his bare, muscular back to her. His bronze shoulder rose above the patchwork quilt she had lent him. One dark-haired arm was tucked beneath the pillow; the other rested across his lean waist. His deep, even breathing convinced her he was asleep.

Disappointment coursed through her. *He needs his rest*, she told herself.

Quietly, she rounded the cot to his other side and peered down into his face. She took in his dark lashes, the black hair framing his angular face, the cleft chin and wide, firm lips. His male beauty entranced her. And the elusive scent of his skin and hair—musky, masculine, uniquely his— deepened her sensual longing.

She wondered what he'd do if she kissed him. Sudden doubts flurried through her. Years had passed since they had last made love. She had been eighteen then; she was twenty-eight now. Would he still find her desirable?

She paced away from him and struggled to rid herself of the doubts. Boost her confidence. Regain the certainty she had felt so strongly back there during her lily-scented bath.

When she turned back toward him, she froze. His eyes were open. And he was staring at her.

8

NOTHING COULD HAVE prepared her for the stark astonishment in those gray eyes. Ryan braced himself on his forearm, and drew his dark brows together.

All her rationalizing about truth and honesty fled in the embarrassment of the moment. For the first time in her life, shyness struck Sunny speechless.

Staring, Ryan tossed the quilt aside and stood up. His broad, muscular chest was smooth and bare, tapering down to a lean waist above maroon silk pajama bottoms. His shiny dark hair was tousled from sleep. He looked like a jungle animal suddenly roused from slumber. Wary. Dangerous.

Incredibly sexy.

Anticipation spiraled through her. She wanted him. She wanted to feel his hands on her, to taste his kiss.

The gentle May breeze rippled the lace curtains, a dusky lock of Ryan's hair, the sheer folds of Sunny's gown. Outside, crickets chirped and a dog barked. Night birds called.

Inside, silence stretched between them.

Ryan wondered if he was awake. Or was this all just another of those dreams that tormented him every time he slept.

"Ryan?" Sunny whispered.

His astonishment grew. This wasn't a dream. There'd be no question in her voice and eyes in any dream of his. *What the hell was she wearing?*

With his fist on his hip, Ryan ambled in a dazed half circle around her, his gaze making a slow descent. Ivory lace against golden flesh; full, rose tipped breasts barely veiled; tantalizing curves, shadowed valleys. She was round and full, sleek and flat, an angel—a beautiful, temptress angel—within an arm's reach. *An angel that should have been his.* A deep-seated frustration grew inside him along with a stirring heat in his loins.

"Why the hell are you wearing that in front of me?"

Sunny jumped at his fierce question. Shocked, she realized the glitter in his gray eyes and the tension in his jaw were not caused by desire, but by anger. She had wanted truth; now she had it. The intimacy they'd shared in the past meant nothing. She was his employee—*only* his employee—and he obviously intended to keep it that way.

Never had she felt so humiliated. She choked out, "Sorry I woke you." Blindly, she turned away from him.

In a half stride, Ryan blocked her path. "Sorry's not good enough. I've been sleeping on a damned cot instead of in the bed to make sure I don't do anything *improper* in my sleep." His dark eyes flashed as his thunderous disapproval rumbled through her. "What gives you the right to strut around half-naked?"

Mutinous pride kept her from crossing her arms and running for cover. "I'm not strutting around," she said with stiff-lipped dignity. "And I'm not half-naked."

"You damn sure are." Again his eyes traveled over her body in a glowering path. Chill bumps tingled everywhere his gaze touched. "And it's worse than naked, Sunny. A hell of a lot worse."

Her chin came up, even as her heart plummeted. *He truly didn't want her.* "If you don't like what I'm wearing, go back to sleep." She tried to sidestep him on her way to the bathroom.

He grabbed her by the shoulders, and she felt the iron control he was having to exert. "Don't you ever tease me again," he warned through clenched teeth.

Sunny's eyebrows shot up and her lips parted in surprise. "You think I'm teasing you?"

"It might be a game to you," he growled, his temper flaring hotter with every word, "but it's not to me."

"Ryan! I never intended—"

"You didn't *accidentally* slip into this damned negligee."

"No," she said on a gasp, twisting her shoulders beneath his tightening grip. "Of course not. But I—"

"But nothing." His hands moved from her lace-covered shoulders to her bare upper arms. "I want you too damned much to pretend not to notice."

Breathlessly, she whispered, "You do?"

Ryan swallowed a groan. Her gaze had gone all soft and sultry. Was she taunting him? He knew he should drop his hands from her and walk away, but the beauty of her eyes and hair and luxuriant body infused him with a deep ache. "You know I do."

Sunny's hand crept up to the ties between her full, high breasts and she tugged at the knots. The lacy edges of the gown's bodice slowly parted.

His breathing, his heartbeat, his universe, stilled.

"Was that an accident, Ry?" she whispered.

Ryan searched her tempestuous green eyes—deeply, desperately—evaluating her intent. "It better not be, Sunny," he hoarsely uttered, "because I'm not going to stop."

And just in case she meant to back away, he tangled his fingers in her hair, drew her irresistibly to him and kissed her with the savage force of his desire.

Yes, he thought. *Yes.* She was sweetness, smooth as honey. A sweetness he'd been craving far too long. She was excitement, and adventure, and a bone-deep pleasure that fired him straight to the top of the world, then down for a gut-level thrill.

But the kiss went on, beyond the familiar. And his ability to think exploded in the need to possess her. All of her. Entirely.

He swept the loosened gown from her shoulders, down her slender back and curvacious hips, until the soft, diaphanous fabric pooled at her feet.

The sudden skin-to-skin contact of her breasts against his chest intensified Sunny's ardor. She reveled in his kiss, in the sensuous demand of his lips, the domination of his muscled embrace, the sultry taste of his mouth....

He moved from her lips to brush kisses along her throat, each one sending languid heat to every part of her body. His kisses slowed into hot swirls of his tongue, down past her collarbone, to the sensitive inner curves of her breasts. He circled and tasted each hardened bud. Sunny trembled in reaction.

Ryan groaned and pulled away long enough to utter, "Protection. Have to get—"

She pressed the foil packet into his hand. Surprise glittered in his eyes as he took it. Urgently, then, he fumbled with the packet, as she pushed his pajama bottoms down to his muscle-corded thighs. Together they dove into another kiss—deep, deeper, straining to reach a treasure hidden somewhere inside the other.

With a low, primal moan, Ryan grasped the back of her thighs and hoisted her from the floor. He meant to carry her to the bed. But gone was the teenaged virgin he had seduced, the girl he had mesmerized with passion. In her place was a woman, explosively responsive in his arms.

Her long, slim legs wrapped around his hips, and she arched herself against his urgent hardness.

His breath came in hot rushes. Her body transformed into fluid motion. He forgot about carrying her to the bed.

Their rhythm quickened; moans turned into gasps. She strained downward. He thrust up. His hardness probed, again and again, but her tightness impeded his entry. Slowing his movement, he determinedly entered her. And forced her down, down, to engulf him.

A surprised cry escaped Sunny as intense pleasure penetrated regions of her heart she never knew existed. When she thought his pulsating love had filled her to capacity, he gave another smooth, urgent thrust.

And for a white-hot, searing second, neither breathed, locked in ultimate closeness. Then he moved...the slightest move...and erotic shock waves convulsed them. Fused them, into one.

Sunny's vision blurred with the heat. Tears stung beneath her lids. She had known their lovemaking would be beautiful. But never, not even in the frenzied passion of their youth, had it ever felt so right.

They fell sideways onto the bed, trembling in each other's arms. Flesh to flesh, heartbeat to heartbeat. Emotion surged through Sunny with a pressure that forced words to her tongue. Dangerous, forbidden words. *I love you. I love you.* She didn't say them. Didn't even want to think them. It's the old hormone thing, she told herself. Chemistry, as Ryan had always said.

You are not in love with him. And he's not in love with you. With painful clarity, she remembered his ferocious response all those years ago when she, on the brink of losing her virginity, had whispered, "Do you love me?"

His instantaneous anger had frightened her. "I won't play mind games with you, Sunny, and you won't play mind games with me. I want you. I might just die if you say no. But if you're looking for more than that, walk away from me now."

She hadn't walked away. She had given in to his hot, wild kisses and made love to him all summer long. And when the time of reckoning came, he accepted responsibility without hesitation. He'd been there for her and their unborn baby.

But he had never changed his mind about love. His comment during their picnic had confirmed that. "Show me a miserable human being, and I'll show you a victim of emotional dependence." He hadn't even wanted to say the "L" word.

Lying there now in the warmth of his arms, Sunny wondered what had happened in his life to turn him so fiercely against love. It was almost as if someone had broken his heart, long before he had become romantically involved with her. But no one had, as far as she knew. At the age of twenty, he hadn't let anyone close enough.

Maybe he'd been right about love all the while, Sunny reflected. Maybe it *was* just a mind game. When she thought about her mother's many marriages—all for the sake of "love"— and the heartbreak she herself had suffered when her own marriage had ended, she could see what Ryan had meant.

So get your wits together, she commanded herself. If she couldn't, she'd have to walk away now. But as Ryan nuzzled the side of her neck, mumbled something unintelligible and molded her body to his, she discarded all thoughts of walking away.

The hormone thing had always been enough for Ryan. This time, it would be enough for her, too. And if contrary feelings bubbled up inside her now and then—as they were right now— she'd never, ever let him know.

SOMETHING PULLED RYAN from his deep sleep.

Sunny's body was no longer entwined with his. Awareness of her had stayed with him while he slept, like glowing embers warming a near-darkened hearth. But now he sensed her absence, and felt cold.

He opened his eyes, and searched the sunlit room. Sunny wasn't in it. The depth of his disappointment startled him.

The one thing he'd missed almost as much as her lovemaking had been the tender hours they'd spent in the early mornings, holding each other, warm and naked. Never, not even after their worst quarrels, had she lain separately from him in the morning.

Until recently, of course. As in, the past ten years.

Reality flooded him, like a bright white light, dispelling the illusions of the night before. What had he done? *He'd made love to Sunny.* Cursing beneath his breath, Ryan swung his feet to the floor and bounded out of bed.

It had been a stupid thing to do.

He snatched his robe from the closet on his way to the bathroom, cursing himself with every step. He should have known better. He should have been stronger.

Opening the immaculate white shower stall, he turned the water on full blast and stepped under the spray. He'd been a damned fool. Making love to Sunny wasn't a quick, harmless roll in the hay. It was more like flirting with fire. A wildfire that could rage out of control in the blink of an eye.

He knew that much from experience. One kiss that summer long ago, and he'd become obsessed. All he could think about had been Sunny. Everything else in his life could have gone to hell— *had* gone to hell—and he hadn't cared. But he'd been a boy then. Almost as naive as Sunny had been at the time.

Not so now. *He* controlled his world now—with rational thought, not passion. *He* set the pace in whatever races he chose to run, whatever mountains he chose to climb. He lit—and extinguished—his passion when and where he chose to.

And from what he had learned recently about Sunny, she now controlled her world. The passive young ingenue was gone.

The hot, punishing stream of water beating against his face helped calm Ryan somewhat. And he began to remember the details of last night.

She had approached him wearing a transparent negligee. And holding a condom. Even now, he could barely believe it, that she had intended for them to make love.

Why? For the mere carnal pleasure of it?

It was possible, he supposed. He couldn't deny the damned hormonal thing between them was just as strong—no, stronger!—than it had been years before. Just remembering her kisses and the passion of last night was enough to get him worked up again.

He couldn't remember sex *ever* having been as good.

So then why hadn't she stayed with him this morning?

Uttering a violent oath, Ryan gritted his teeth and turned the water knob to cold. He had a feeling he would need quite a few cold showers before he finished this business with Sunny.

And finish it, he would. As quickly as possible, *without* a repeat of last night. Because no matter how lightly Ms. Liberated might take their relationship, he wasn't about to chance being burned again. By anyone.

He'd stick to women who couldn't burn him if they tried.

LAVINIA, LOOKING ELEGANT in a designer dress of black on white, with matching pumps and earrings, her dark brown curls impeccably styled, met Ryan in the Oak Hall at the foot of the Grand Staircase. "Thank goodness you're up. I was about to call your room. Where's Sunny?"

Ryan frowned. "She isn't down here already?"

"I saw her earlier," Lavinia replied, "when she set up the breakfast buffet on the sun porch. A lovely idea. The guests have been raving with compliments over the change. I should have thought of it myself. I haven't seen her since."

"Ah, excuse me," interrupted Mrs. Lee, "but Mrs. Alexander went out with her sketch pad. Said she was going to draw."

"Oh, dear," moaned Lavinia, looking worried. "I hope she returns in time."

"In time for what?" asked Ryan.

"The news crew is on its way."

"News crew?" he repeated with a sinking feeling.

"A local television station picked up on the rescue story. They want to interview Jonathon, Sunny and you."

"This hero thing is crazy," protested Ryan. "I did what anyone would have."

"Your modesty is charming, Ryan, but you must emphasize the fact that the boy *climbed over a fence* to get to that ledge. A tall fence, with warning signs. Any slur against our safety standards will hurt our business. And technically, he was trespassing, since he wasn't a guest of ours. But of course, we won't mention that unless it becomes absolutely necessary."

"I'd rather not be interviewed at all."

"But you must! This could give Windsong Place a nice publicity boost. A touch of human interest. If they can find Grady for an interview, the show might be aired nationally. It would cost us thousands to get that kind of exposure."

Anxiety tightened Ryan's chest. He didn't like public exposure. On the other hand, bad publicity would hurt the inn he was about to purchase.

"'Morning, there, Alexander," greeted Wilbur from behind him. "Sorry I was so late getting back from town last night. Sounds like you had a lot of excitement while I was gone."

"Oh, it was exciting, all right," responded Ryan. "Did you bring the purchase agreement for me?"

"Sure did. After this interview business is over, you can come up to my suite and we'll go over the details."

Ryan immediately cheered up. The light shone at the end of the tunnel—the purchase agreement was ready to sign. Nothing could have made him happier.

Lavinia invited him to a quick breakfast, but as they made their way to the glassed-in side porch where Sunny had set up the breakfast buffet, the news crew arrived.

The next hour was pandemonium. The inn quickly came alive with fast-moving cameramen, technicians with lighting equipment and administrative aides carrying clipboards. Curious guests gathered in clusters to watch.

In the midst of it all, the richly carved front entrance swung open and Sunny entered, clutching her sketch pad to her chest. She wore short denim cutoffs and an oversize peach knit top that had slipped slightly down one tanned shoulder beneath her windblown golden curls. Professor Collins accompanied her. Both of them stopped in obvious surprise at the commotion in the Oak Hall.

Her green-eyed gaze met Ryan's, and from across the crowded room, he wondered if he knew her at all. He didn't believe so. Because even though he could have correctly answered a thousand questions about her past, he couldn't even guess at what she was thinking or feeling right now. Her gaze was as neutral as a stranger's would have been. Why had she initiated their lovemaking last night? Did she regret it now? He found himself wanting to know.

"There's Sunny!" cried Lavinia, bustling over to her. Hooking a hand around her arm, Lavinia ushered her to Ryan's side. "You stand right here, dear, next to Ryan, until they tell you what to do." She whispered to them both, "Think PR."

At this close range, Sunny did not meet Ryan's gaze, which he found interesting. And disturbing.

The smartly dressed blond anchorwoman introduced herself and rattled off instructions about speaking clearly and facing the camera, then explained that they'd be interviewing Jonathon first, and hopefully his father; they were expected any moment.

Lights were being erected and adjusted around a grouping of wing chairs beside the fireplace when Jonathon Barrett charged in. To Ryan, he cried, "I'm gonna be on television! So are you. You'll tell them, won't you? About the Cullowhee lily I found?" Excitement blazed in his freckled face.

"*You* tell them," responded Ryan. "I think you're first."

"But they might not believe me."

Sunny opened her sketch book and carefully withdrew a sheet of paper. "Here. This is for you."

Jonathon took it and studied it with solemn interest. "It's my lily," he said in a wonder-filled tone. "On the cliff." He looked at Sunny, and his smile warmed even Ryan's heart. "I can show them now!" He jumped up and down, his straight, reddish brown hair bouncing. "Wait until my pa sees it!"

He then caught sight of Professor Collins and ran over to show him the picture. "I found it, Professor! A Cullowhee lily!"

"Yes, yes, I saw your lily this morning," rumbled the professor, his eyes sparkling, his pipe firmly between his teeth. "It certainly looks like a Cullowhee. Remarkable find."

Ryan realized that Sunny had taken the professor up to Devil's Ridge. To authenticate Jonathon's find. This was the Sunny he knew—the deeply caring Sunny. An emotion flashed through him, warm and troublesome, but like a shooting star, it faded quickly before he could see it clearly.

Technicians positioned Jonathon in an armchair, where he proudly displayed the picture of his flower. Professor Collins stood expostulating about the rarity of Cullowhee lilies, and the possibility that the boy's find was genuine.

"Alexander, old buddy!"

A deep, melodious voice with a country twang spun Ryan around to face the front door. Golden-haired Grady Barrett swaggered toward them wearing a black Stetson, black shirt, buckskin vest and jeans. Charisma and energy glowed from his amber eyes. Although Grady had acquired an undeniable suavity along with his fame, his grin remained the same as when they were kids—hell-bent on mischief.

According to the tabloids, Ryan's old pal still lived for fun, though his taste in "fun" now seemed to revolve around sexual conquest. Ryan couldn't imagine him as a father.

They shook hands and Grady patted Ryan on the back. "You saved my son's life, buddy. I owe you."

"You owe that boy more."

Grady let the rebuke pass. "So is it true? Can you really be *married?*" Astonishment glittered in his eyes. "I heard something about a Mrs. Alexander."

Conscious of the crowd gaping more at them now than at the television interview of Jonathon, Ryan regarded Grady in dismay. "We'll talk later."

"So where's your bride?" Grady's amber gaze then fell on Sunny. "Sunny! Is that you? Good lord, it's been ... what, nine or ten years? You mean, you two got back together?"

Against all logic, Ryan felt a thrill of possessive pride. His reaction bothered him. Why should he want Grady to think Sunny was his again?

But he did. And not only because of the Tanners' proximity—which was reason enough. Both Lavinia and Wilbur stood a few yards away, watching Jonathon's interview. Fortunately, they hadn't heard Grady's exclamation.

"Lower your voice, Grady," Ryan muttered. "I'd prefer to keep my private life private."

"Yeah, but—"

"It's good to see you again, Grady," cut in Sunny, shaking his hand. Although actually, it wasn't. She had never been particularly fond of him. When they were kids, he hadn't wanted her tagging along, and when she had married Ryan, he hadn't been very approving. Beneath his good-ole-country-boy veneer, Grady had always been somewhat of a snob. Both he and Ryan were sons of an elite, moneyed society. They had attended expensive boarding schools and associated with well-pedigreed friends. She did not belong to that world. With Grady, she had always felt like an outsider.

But now he treated her to his famous heartthrob smile. "You're looking as pretty as ever. Glad to see things worked out." Clapping Ryan on the back, he said, "This here fella needs a good woman to settle him down. When did you two make up? I never thought I'd see the day—"

"We'll talk about old times later," insisted Ryan. "Right now, your son is about to make his television debut."

Surprised, Grady glanced over the heads of bystanders to where Jonathon was responding to the anchorwoman's questions. Grady turned to Ryan, his manner subdued, his voice lowered. "They're going to interview me next. I need your help here, old buddy."

Ryan raised his brows in silent question.

In an embarrassed undertone, Grady explained, "My ex-wife is trying to get custody of Jonathon. She wants control of his trust fund. Her lawyers would love to get hold of some so-called evidence of neglect on my part."

"What does this have to do with me?" asked Ryan.

"Make it clear that he disobeyed his nanny, who was there with him the entire time."

Sunny bit the inside of her cheek to stop from protesting. To portray Jonathon in that light, even though it might be technically accurate, seemed like a betrayal. She wondered why Grady wanted custody of the son he rarely bothered to see.

From Ryan's blank expression, Sunny guessed he shared her view. "Sorry, buddy. I've said all I'm going to say."

Grady stared at him, looking surprised and hurt.

From across the crowded room, Jonathon cried, "There's my pa!" His tone implied even greater awe than he had expressed over the Cullowhee lily. The sheer adoration in his eyes caught at Sunny's heart. His cheeks were flushed with anticipation as Grady advanced through the crowd.

Jonathon's thin shoulders straightened. The wide armchair emphasized his smallness; his black, high-topped sneakers dangled far above the Oriental carpet. He held the picture of his treasured flower in both hands, waiting in taut readiness for his chance to shine.

Wait until I show my pa, he had said.

The television cameras swung to focus on the approaching celebrity. Grady adopted a paternal smile and advanced to his son's side. Jonathon's face beamed in an answering grin. "Hi, Pa! I'm on TV," he whispered loudly as Grady sat beside him.

The crowd around him chuckled.

Be impressed, Sunny silently prayed. *Be proud*.

In a polished tone he might have used on stage, Grady queried, "Do you know why you're on television, son?"

Jonathon nodded, his red-brown eyes sparkling. "Because I found a Cullowhee lily."

"No, Jonathon," his father contradicted him. "You're on television because a man saved your life."

Jonathon tilted his head in obvious confusion. His father hadn't even glanced at the drawing he held.

Warming up to his role, Grady went on in a stern voice, "Do you know why he had to do that?"

Sunny's heart dropped as the boy's face went pale. He shook his head no. The freckles on his nose stood out in stark relief against his pale skin.

Grady spoke in the righteous manner of television-show fathers delivering a well-deserved rebuke. "Because you ran away from your nanny. You forgot everything I've taught you about safety in the mountains. I think you owe your nanny, and Mr. Alexander, an apology."

Jonathon hung his head. After a terrible pause—one that seemed to last forever—he turned to where Ryan stood in the crowd. In a small, trembling whisper, he said, "I'm sorry."

Someone yelled "Cut." The bright lights and cameras clicked off. Jonathon's interview was over.

The desolation on the child's face propelled Sunny beyond prudence. She cut through the crowd until she faced Grady Barrett. "Perhaps your attitude would change, Grady, if you understood *why* Jonathon climbed that fence marked Danger."

Grady looked up at her in surprise.

"If you'd listen to his explanation, you might understand how important that lily was to him. His nanny didn't understand, but maybe, just maybe, *you* would have." A tightness restricted Sunny's throat and made each word painful. "But you weren't there. And now that you are, you refuse to listen."

Seeing Grady's affronted look, she knew she should stop, but couldn't. "He wanted to share with you something special and rare and ... and ... magic." She added in a strangled whisper, "He said you'd be proud he found it."

The futility of Jonathon's longing seared her. Both she and Ryan had lived through the same kind of thwarted yearning. "The only reason he let Ryan pull him up the cliff without that flower was so that it wouldn't die." Through a glimmering sheen, she saw only a blur. "Another thing you should be proud of."

The ache in Sunny's chest had grown too painful. She whirled around and forced her way through the crowd in a blind rush for the front door.

The cool air outside did little to abate the stinging in her eyes and throat. She flew down the front stairway through the azalea garden and across the circular drive to the silent woods beyond. Shivering in the brisk morning breeze, she wrapped her arms around herself and struggled not to cry.

What did a person have to do to earn love? The question had always baffled her. As a child, she had assumed adults knew. But questions of love mystified her more now than ever.

Steady, purposeful footsteps sounded on the walkway behind her. She didn't turn around. She knew who had followed her; she had developed a kind of sixth sense where Ryan was concerned.

"Sunny?" His gentle, deep-timbred voice somehow increased the trembling of her bottom lip. She swallowed hard.

He encircled her from behind with strong arms and held her tightly against his chest until she could feel the forceful beating of his heart through his denim shirt. His chin rested against her ear.

Weren't these the arms she had sought as a child when overcome by an uncaring world? Hadn't she weathered countless storms in his embrace, clinging as if he were her lifeboat?

So why should she be afraid to turn to him now?

But she was. She could no sooner turn and cry in his arms than she could fly to Pluto. Things weren't that simple anymore.

"I've really done it now," she said. "I've alienated one of Windsong Place's most influential neighbors. I may have alienated Lavinia, too, and probably ruined the resort's publicity."

Ryan turned her around to face him. "You said what needed to be said. I don't know how you do it, Sunny, but sometimes what I'm feeling comes out of your mouth."

Gazing up at him, she wanted to say *I love you*. She caught herself just in time. Gathering her strength around her like a shield, she reminded herself that it was only chemistry between them. Pure chemistry. He wasn't thinking about love.

"God, Sunny, don't look at me like that," Ryan whispered. He recognized that look, and it cut through him like a death-cold chill. She was shutting him out. Turning off her warmth. He'd fought that battle—and lost—in the days before she'd left him.

Beneath his pensive scrutiny, Sunny stiffened, her heart tripping over itself. He had read her feelings. He knew she was falling in love with him again. But she wasn't. She wouldn't. "I don't know what you're talking about, Ryan."

His teeth clenched. "I don't want to go through this again with you, Sunny."

No, of course he wouldn't. He never had wanted her love. Answering anger rose in her, and she turned away from him.

He caught her shoulder. "Why did you want to make love to me last night?"

"I thought it'd be fun," she responded, intentionally flip.

"Fun?" he repeated.

Afraid to subject herself to his disturbing scrutiny much longer, she abruptly turned and strode out of the shielding forest, back toward the house.

Ryan angrily followed her across the circular drive. As they neared the house, a ponytailed man with a video camera and the anchorwoman met them at the foot of the garden stairway with a microphone.

Lavinia accompanied them. "They'd like to tape your segment here, in front of the inn. You know, as an introduction to the piece." To Sunny, she whispered, "No more outbursts, hmmm?"

As Sunny struggled to regain her composure, the anchorwoman posed herself beside Ryan and spoke with professional clarity. "We're here at Windsong Place, a

Victorian mansion in the North Carolina mountains, where technology tycoon Ryan Alexander risked his life to rescue the young son of country singer Grady Barrett from Devil's Ridge, a treacherous precipice."

Lavinia leaned forward and commandeered the microphone. "Yes, here we are, with our very own heroes, the new franchise owners of Windsong Place...Mr. and Mrs. Ryan Alexander."

At that, Sunny and Ryan overcame their differences long enough to exchange an appalled glance. *Mr. and Mrs. On national television!*

But the worst was yet to come. No sooner had the interview ended than a spry elderly lady pushed her way to the front of the crowd. "Hold your horses just one dad-blasted moment," she said fiercely, her age-spotted fists on her hips. "I want to know what in the tarnation is going on here."

In utter horror, Sunny stared into the irate face of her grandmother.

9

"*OLIVE,*" GROANED RYAN.

"Don't you try to smooth-talk your way past me, you...you back stabber." The petite, gray-haired woman wore a pink warm-up suit, tiny pearl earrings and white sneakers; she blasted him with her green-eyed glare. "You deadbeat defiler of women!"

"It's nice to see you, too, Olive," he murmured, casting an eye at the listening crowd. "Why don't we step inside and finish this conversation?"

"We ain't going nowhere until I get some answers, boy." And even though Lavinia, Wilbur, the anchorwoman and the crowd gaped openmouthed, Ryan wasn't the least bit surprised by her attack. Olive hadn't spoken a soft word to him in her life. She'd called him "boy" until he was thirteen and told her not to. She'd made him stand in the corner for hours when he misbehaved, and whenever Sunny hurt herself playing, Olive had always placed the blame squarely on his shoulders.

She had also forced him to eat his vegetables, taken him on fishing trips, taught him to hold his own in a mean game of poker and insisted on accompanying him to mother-son functions at his school. And whenever he had needed her, Olive had been there. She had never left him.

Tough, she was. Tough as cinnamon cookies.

Her wide-set green eyes shot sparks at him now, reminding him very much of her granddaughter. "Mr. and

Mrs. Alexander, my foot," she spat. "You two are no more married than I am."

"Grandma!" Sunny's cheeks blazed with embarrassment as she firmly took hold of the old woman's arm. "You're making a spectacle of yourself. We will discuss this matter in private."

Olive yanked her arm out of Sunny's grasp. "Don't try to pull the wool over my eyes, girl. I talked to you Friday, and you weren't married then. You were on a business trip, you said. Bah! You were busy being lured down the road to ruin by this smooth talker. *Again!*"

Grady strolled up out of the crowd to stand beside Olive. "They forgot to invite *me* to their wedding too, Miz Olive."

"Mind your own business, Grady," snapped Olive. "If you had, that boy of yours wouldn't have needed rescuing."

Grady paled and shut his mouth. Ryan sympathized. Olive's tongue-lashing had left grooves in his own pride many times. He had a feeling this was going to be another one of those times.

Lavinia, who had been blocking the camera lens in case the cameraman started shooting, found her voice. "You're Sunny's grandmother?" she chimed in welcoming tones, her smile just a little forced. "Welcome to Windsong Place. Ryan, Sunny, help your grandmother up these stairs. We'll have tea inside."

"I haven't come here for tea," muttered Olive, but Ryan and Sunny had already trapped her between them and she wasn't about to lose her dignity by struggling. Holding her head high, she marched up the garden steps as if it had been her idea.

A man with a camera stepped out from behind a column on the front porch, clicking photos as they passed.

Ryan recognized him as a paparazzo from the tabloid that had exploited him before.

As they escorted Olive to the private parlor located beyond the formal dining room, Lavinia issued orders to Wilbur to keep their other guests—and the media—occupied until they could resolve this "unfortunate misunderstanding."

In the chintz-decorated parlor, Olive reluctantly settled onto the love seat with Sunny. Ryan swung the heavy oak door closed but Lavinia intercepted it and stepped inside to join them. Ryan and Sunny exchanged another speaking glance. Things couldn't get much worse, or could they?

"What's this all about?" demanded Lavinia curtly, her smooth social polish giving way to steely eyes and an acid tone.

"You stay out of it, missy," ordered Olive, pointing an arthritic finger at Lavinia. Lavinia stiffened and pursed her lips. Ryan rubbed his palm over his face.

"That's enough, Grandma," Sunny scolded. "We didn't tell you about our marriage because we wanted to surprise you."

"You sure as hell did that. And not in a good way, either. He broke your heart before, and he'll break it again."

Ryan frowned. "I never did anything to hurt Sunny."

"You must have, because that's the only way she would have left you. It took her years to get over you. *If* she ever did."

Ryan's eyes flickered to Sunny in surprise, but she avoided his gaze, focusing on Olive. "I've told you a million times, Grandma, none of that is true. Ryan and I parted ways—" she gave a quick look at Lavinia "—for a while . . . because we were too young at the time to know what we wanted. But we're older now, and you have to trust us enough to let us handle our own . . . affairs." Her cheeks blazed at the last word. Ryan closed his eyes tightly. This couldn't be happening. Windsong Place was slipping further out of his reach with every word spoken.

"You look me straight in the eye, Sunny," demanded Olive, "and tell me you've already married him. And if you have, I'll keep my mouth shut and butt out of your business."

Pinning her honesty on a mere technicality, Sunny stared her grandmother straight in the eye. "I've already married him, Grandma." *Ten years ago*, she silently added. "And you don't have to worry. My relationship with Ryan is better now—" her gaze shifted to Ryan "—just as it is than it has ever been before," she said emphatically.

Ryan got the message, loud and clear. No matter how many times they made love, she would never be his again. What they had shared last night had been sex. Just sex. Nothing more.

"I hope you know what you're doing," grumbled Olive. "But I'm afraid you're counting on something that just ain't there. Ryan's heart was torn right out of him long before you met him."

Both Ryan and Sunny narrowed their eyes on her then, waiting for her to say more, but the color had drained from Olive's wrinkled face. Sunny reached for her in concern. "Grandma—?"

"I'm okay," she murmured.

"I'll go see what's keeping the tea," Lavinia said.

"I don't need any tea," Olive retorted weakly. "A strong belt of schnapps would do me better."

The parlor door opened and a young, red-haired woman with friendly eyes entered. "There you are," she said reprovingly to Olive. "When we found your room empty, I figured this is where you'd be." To Sunny, she explained, "That article about you in the newspaper today got her pretty riled up."

Olive scowled, crossed her arms and stuck her bottom lip out. "I can visit my granddaughter if I want to."

"You know you're not supposed to leave the hospital yet. And you sure aren't supposed to be driving," the woman scolded. "Doc Langley won't like it when he finds out you took his car."

Olive's spunk revived. "Tom Langley don't own that car, his rich wife does. And she'd rather have me driving it than him carting you pretty nurses all over town."

The nurse blushed redder than her hair and didn't utter another word as she and Sunny helped Olive up from the settee.

On her way past Ryan, Olive halted and laid her weathered palm against his cheek. "It's your last chance to keep her, boy," she warned quietly. "Better not blow it this time."

Then Sunny and the nurse led her out.

"A pity," murmured Lavinia to Ryan, "when they get to that stage. Poor dear's obviously confused."

Ryan didn't think Olive had ever been confused in her life. Outspoken and ornery, yes. But whatever came out of her mouth was usually the untarnished truth.

So why did she think he had done Sunny wrong? And what had she meant about his heart being torn out of him *before* Sunny had come into his life?

With worry in her eyes, Lavinia took hold of Ryan's arm and confided, "*I* know that you and Sunny are married. But the media will have a field day with Olive's outburst. This is the kind of publicity we *don't* want connected to our family resort inns. Our image must remain spotless. Mom and pop . . ."

"And apple pie," Ryan finished dryly.

"Precisely. But don't worry," Lavinia assured him as they made their way toward the front of the house. "I'll put an end to whatever tawdry scandal the media might be brewing, right here and now. If I can't turn a potential disaster into a social triumph, my name's not Lavinia Alcott Mayhew Tanner."

Ryan followed her to the front porch, curious about what she had planned. The crowd milling around on the front lawn had somehow doubled in size. Although the television news crew had gone, the ponytailed cameraman remained with his video camera, and the paparazzo from the tabloid still lurked in the shrubbery.

"Good news," Lavinia announced regally from the front porch, which could have been a stage. "Since Sunny's grandmother missed the wedding ceremony... due to health reasons, you understand—" she paused to let her explanation sink in "—they have decided to renew their vows. We'll hold the ceremony right here, Saturday morning, in the rose gardens of Windsong Place."

Ryan turned to Lavinia with a disbelieving stare.

Sunny froze in the driveway after waving goodbye to her grandmother's departing car.

Oblivious to the couple's less-than-enthusiastic response, Lavinia continued with a gracious smile, "The guests of Windsong Place are invited to share in the celebration, of course, as well as members of the media who are present here today."

Cameras clicked. The crowd cheered. Ryan silently vowed to strangle Olive the next time he saw her.

DIRECTLY AFTER her announcement, Lavinia enlisted Sunny's help in planning Saturday morning's ceremony. They'd need flowers to decorate the gazebo, a wedding cake, champagne, punch and hors d'oeuvres—only the best, of course. The list seemed endless, and impossible to achieve in only six days.

But Lavinia insisted the ceremony be performed as promised. "The public loves weddings. Especially society weddings. We'll tell reporters that you married suddenly in a brief civil ceremony, without your families in attendance because you were too much in love to wait. But now, you're holding the ceremony to please your dear old grandmother. It's perfect. I love it."

Sunny did *not* love it. This ceremony would be the crowning mockery of their true relationship. But their true relationship didn't enter into it. Only appearances mattered. From the few words they'd managed to share, she knew Ryan felt it would cause less of a stir to go along with the plans than to disrupt them. It couldn't hurt anything, he'd muttered. The ceremony would involve no legalities. Nothing binding in the eyes of the law. Just words and gestures performed for an audience. Just an extension of the performance they'd been giving for the last few days.

"Would you like to write your own vows?" suggested Lavinia, her eyes sparkling at the idea.

"No," snapped Sunny and Ryan in resounding unison.

"The traditional ceremony will be fine," added Sunny. The less they had to say, the better.

Ryan and Wilbur spent the rest of the day contending with the unexpected crowd that had converged on Windsong Place. From the size of it, Sunny judged the entire population of Heaven's Hollow had come to investigate the happening in their tiny community, along with a group of ambitious paparazzi intent on building the events of the day into a sensational scoop.

When most of the curiosity-seekers had left, both Ryan and Sunny fielded a flurry of phone calls from friends and

acquaintances who had seen the broadcast and couldn't
believe they had married. By mutual agreement, they both
lied through their teeth. Their marriage, they told every
caller, had been a sudden one. Yes, they'd be renewing
their vows on Saturday.

It wasn't until evening that Sunny escaped to the privacy of the bedroom. Ryan made his way upstairs shortly
after.

He bolted the door, then drew the vertical blinds over
the French doors and windows, just in case ambitious paparazzi resorted to climbing trees.

Unaware of his arrival, Sunny stepped out of the steamy
bathroom, freshly showered and wrapped in a fluffy white
bath towel. For an awkward moment, they found themselves facing each other. Alone. In the bedroom where
they had made love.

His gaze left hers and flickered downward—in a brief
glance that seemed to take in all of her, from her wet, glis-
tening shoulders, to the damp, tightly wrapped towel, to
her long, bare legs. Her pulse quickened, and the towel
seemed to grow smaller with each second that ticked by.

"I didn't know you were here." She tucked the corner
of the towel between her breasts to secure it. Determined
to hide her tension, she resolved to go about her business
as usual. She strolled to the closet with deliberate nonchalance.

Through the vanity mirror, she saw him brace his hand
against the doorframe of the dressing room. His silver-
gray gaze followed her. Or rather, followed the sway of her
hips.

Reaction spiraled through her. Warm, unwanted reaction to his palpable, virile power. She didn't want to be
alone with him right now. Her feelings were too raw and
jumbled, and dangerously close to the surface. She needed

a little quiet time alone to hammer her defenses solidly back into place.

I don't want to go through this again with you, Sunny, he had said. Forcing her teeth to unclench, she busied herself by riffling through the closet for her nightshirt. A particularly unromantic nightshirt, with cartoon characters on it.

"You realize we've been presented to the entire nation as husband and wife," he said.

"Just another act among many, right? But of course, the national publicity will certainly cramp your style." She shook her head in mock sympathy, which sent a fine spray flying from her wet ringlets. "I can almost hear the hearts breaking in yacht clubs all across America."

After a surprised moment, he answered with an edge in his voice, "You're the one hunting for a husband. An announcement of marriage might complicate your campaign, wouldn't you say?"

"I am *not* hunting for a husband."

"Oh, yeah," he mocked softly. "That's next on your agenda."

She pressed her lips together and continued searching through the closet. For what, she couldn't remember. She wished she hadn't confided her hope of marrying some day. He made it sound so childish, so *gauche*.

"That's not what I want to talk to you about, anyway," he muttered, sounding disgusted with himself. He crossed his muscular arms over his chest and stared at her with the surliness of a mountain bear.

"I'm not really in the mood to talk."

She saw a shimmer of humor—and something much more provocative—momentarily warm his eyes. "I could think of things I'd rather do right now, too." The sensuality of his drawl sent a warm shiver through her. "But there's something I need to know. Why does Olive think I broke your heart?"

Sunny gave up groping through the closet and slammed the door shut. Of all the things he could have brought up, this was possibly the worst. He *had* broken her heart—shattered it into a million pieces. Because he hadn't wanted her love, and he never would.

She knew where this discussion would lead. He would talk about the feelings he had read in her eyes today. He was going to "let her down gently," so to speak, to spare her further heartbreak. She didn't think her pride could stand it.

She turned to face him, her defenses strong. "Let me set your mind at ease. First of all, when it comes to my heart, Olive doesn't have a clue. And secondly, just because I went to bed with you last night, don't think I'm head over heels in love with you."

Ryan flushed and stiffened.

Sunny continued in a quiet but passionate tone, "For the past ten years, I have done *what* I want, *when* I want, and *with whom* I want—" she tapped her bare, water-beaded chest above the towel with her index finger as she advanced, insinuating far more action than she had actually seen "—sexually speaking, that is. And love has never entered into it."

Tonelessly, he replied, "I understand that."

"So don't go getting a big head just because I engaged in a little casual sex with you."

"A little casual sex?"

"Yes, casual. I thought we were mature enough to be honest about the physical attraction between us." Even as she said it, her words mocked her. How could she call herself honest?

"I should've known better than to touch you," he said explosively. "Sex with you always leads to some kind of complication."

Sunny flinched. "Not this time. You can bet on that."

"It already has."

Never had she been quite as confused, because it was true. Stopping within inches of him, she whispered as much to herself as to him, "I'm not in love with you, Ryan Brynfield Alexander." The declaration reverberated in the air, hung there like a threatening storm cloud.

"I never said anything about love," he stated flatly.

Which, of course, was also true. And that was the problem, Sunny realized with painful clarity. They stared at each other in tense silence.

The scent of lilies drifted to Ryan from her wet, dark gold hair. Her smooth lips glistened invitingly. Her eyes, fringed with spiky wet lashes, dazzled him with emerald beauty. Yet those same eyes and lips were staunchly denying any feeling for him whatsoever.

He turned away from her, so filled with anger he was nearly choking on it. She had allowed him a taste of her warmth, just enough to get him obsessing about her again, and now she was shutting him out in the cold. Just as she had ten years ago.

So, then, why did he still want her? As furious as he was, he had to physically restrain himself from tugging that towel off of her and doing his damnedest to revive the warmth her words and eyes denied him.

"Put something on," he ordered.

"Do you want me to leave?" she asked between stiff lips, following him out of the dressing area and into the bedroom.

"Don't put words into my mouth." Ryan realized then with a shock how much he wanted her to stay. "The purchase agreement hasn't been finalized. Do you want to manage the inn, or not?"

"I do."

Relief coursed through him, angering him further with its intensity. "Then you will stay. And we will go through with the ceremony Lavinia promised the media. I'm not going to let Windsong Place slip away from me now."

Sunny shrugged—a deliberately nonchalant agreement to cooperate. She still wore only the towel. Damn her.

Ryan gritted his teeth and fought to regain self-control. He wouldn't touch her again, he swore it. Too much was at stake to have his mind clouded by irrational anger. And explosive desire. Too many serious issues had to be settled.

Which reminded him of an extremely serious issue that had been riding heavily on his mind.

Expelling a long breath, Ryan pulled back one side of the window blind, peered out into darkness and rubbed the back of his neck. "Speaking of complications, there's another subject we need to discuss." He cleared his throat, feeling awkward, which was a totally unfamiliar sensation for him. "Last night. The condom. For some reason, it . . . didn't work."

"What do you mean *didn't work?*"

"It broke. I don't know what I did, but—" He turned and met her gaze.

A vivid blush stained her cheeks and concern shone in her incredibly green eyes. "The condom might have been old," she whispered.

"Were you . . . otherwise protected? Against pregnancy, I mean?"

"Yes, yes, of course."

He frowned in surprise. Not at her answer, but at his gut reaction to it. He should have been relieved, but for the briefest moment, he had been disappointed.

He turned from the window and stared at the roses in the wallpaper, the gleaming brass base of the lamp, the wide, marbled hearth. "Sunny, I swear nothing like this has ever happened before. Since you left me, I haven't been involved with anyone without protection. Secure protection. Against everything." He forced his gaze to hers, but she refused to meet it. "You know how important that is, don't you?"

"Of course."

He crossed his arms and pressed the knuckles of one fist against his chin in silent contemplation. "So how about you? Has this ever happened to you before?"

"No, never," she replied quickly.

His eyes narrowed. "There's something you're not telling me. You're hiding behind some technicality." Slowly he moved toward her. "Do you swear that all those men you've slept with in the past ten years wore condoms?"

Her lips parted; her cheeks blazed. She stammered, "Th-that's none of your business."

"It damn well is." He stopped beside her. "There's a big old wicked world out there, Sunny, and I want to know how much of it I have to worry about."

"You don't have to worry about any of it."

He tipped her chin up with insistent fingers and studied her eyes. "You *have* used protection every time, haven't you?"

Feeling trapped, and terribly vulnerable, she searched for an answer. He was too good at reading her. What could she say that wouldn't be an outright lie? Because she couldn't tell him the truth. She'd die before she'd do that. There had been many men in her life, and a few that she had *slept* with. But none had used protection. Because other than kisses, cuddling and a few stimulating preliminaries, she hadn't made love to any of them.

"Sunny!" Gripping her bare upper arms, Ryan shook her once, twice, his tone growing urgent. "Damn it all to hell, this is serious."

Because she couldn't stand the thought of Ryan fearing to make love to her, she closed her eyes. And died.

"I haven't . . . made love . . . to anyone else."

The answering silence roared in her ears. Although his hands remained wrapped around her arms, she would have otherwise sworn he had disappeared. Vanished.

"Open your eyes," he breathed.

She didn't. She didn't think she could bear it. If she detected even a trace of mockery or amusement, or worse yet, macho chest-beating, she knew she'd shatter into little pieces.

"Open them, I said."

Slowly, fearfully, she obeyed.

She saw flat disbelief in his eyes, but as she held his gaze, the staunch disbelief mellowed into doubt. And slowly, into pure astonishment.

"Don't make anything out of it," Sunny warned, thoroughly mortified. "I've had plenty of dates. Plenty. Two or three a week, sometimes. And they're nice men, all of them. I lead a very full and satisfying social life, really. . . ."

Ryan gently shook her out of her embarrassed rambling. He looked positively shell-shocked. "Why, Sunny? Why?"

She knew what he was asking her. And she answered with the simple truth. "I didn't want any of them."

Slowly, he drew in a breath; his nostrils flaring. His voice, when he finally spoke, was softer than a whisper, thick with awe. "But you came to *me*."

His gaze touched her hair, her mouth, her eyes. "Tell me why."

She swallowed against a sudden dryness in her throat. "Because," she replied in somewhat of a panic, "like you said, sex leads to complications. I wasn't ready to commit myself," she improvised, "and I didn't think it would be fair to . . . lead anyone on." Satisfied with her explanation thus far, she added the final coup de grace. "But with you, I knew there was no danger of either of us getting too serious."

He continued to stare at her.

Desperately she tried to divine his reaction. Had he bought her explanation? Or did he realize that the memory of him had come between her and every other man she'd ever kissed?

His unreadable gaze held her transfixed. "In that case," he said softly, "there's no reason we can't carry on with our . . . casual affair, is there?"

He had called her bluff, and she couldn't back down now. Her blood rushed in her ears, and her every heartbeat hammered a warning. She couldn't have replied if her life depended on it.

"Kiss me, Sunny," he whispered, drawing her to him. Tugging at the towel. "As casual as you want to."

THE TELEPHONE RANG, jarring them both from sleep. Sunny was closest to the phone so she extended an arm from their lover's cocoon of warm, satiny flesh and tangled sheets. The Tuesday morning sun filtered through the lace draperies, dappling the suite with flowerlike patterns of light.

"Yes?" she said into the phone, her voice morning-soft and sleepy. "'Morning, Lavinia."

She lay back against the pillows, smothering a yawn as she listened. "That would be fine," she mumbled from time to time. Movement beneath the covers distracted her. A strong, warm hand glided in a sensuous path around the curve of her hip, across her stomach, up to her breasts. Smiling, she closed her eyes and savored the pleasure coursing through her at his touch. She breathed shakily into the receiver, "Yes, yes, fine."

Teasing caresses across her nipples nearly forced a gasp. Her eyes flew open, and she reached out to capture Ryan's hand, but instead he caught hers and firmly imprisoned it. Covering the mouthpiece, Sunny scolded him in a whisper, "Wait!"

But he didn't. He feathered kisses down the length of her body.

"Whatever you think would work best, Lavinia," Sunny said, forcing herself to remain coherent. As the voice on the phone droned on, she felt the silkiness of Ryan's hair brushing against her leg, then he lightly bit the inside of her thigh. The delicious shock forced the breath from her in an audible rush. Her hand tightened around the receiver. "Lavinia, I'll t-talk to you later," she managed to say before dropping the receiver onto its cradle.

With a throaty moan of surrender, a hot coil of need tightening deep insider her, Sunny closed her eyes and arched her back. Her hips rotated beneath the sheets ever so slowly in a sensuous rhythm. She heard Ryan's deep, masculine groan.

He tossed aside the interfering covers and captured her hips, pressing wet, hot kisses across sensitive mounds and valleys. Her breath caught on a tiny sob.

He tightened his hold and drew his tongue back and forth. Sunny's moans turned to ragged pleas, as she teetered on the brink of pure mindlessness. With a low growl deep in his throat, he invaded her tight, silken warmth with his fingers, and with slow, savoring swirls of his tongue.

Pleasure jolted through her with such intensity, colors flashed beneath her closed eyelids. With a shuddering cry she tangled her fingers in his silky hair and folded herself around him.

Lost in sensual pleasure, she clung to him convulsively, her lips parted and her eyes closed. She struggled to keep him still, for his slightest move sent shock waves rocketing through her.

After a moment, he freed himself of her hold, and his dark face swam before her, his silvery eyes half-lidded with passion.

She saw there an urgent need. He pinned her beneath him. She lifted her hips to meet him, and he staked his claim. Her muscles tightened around him, drawing him deeper in, staking a claim of her own.

THAT MORNING, they did not speak of their sexual odyssey; each of them went about the business of daily living as if nothing out of the ordinary had occurred. But it had. And every chance gaze or incidental touch sent a charge of awareness pulsing between them.

After a cold morning shower that reassured Ryan his soul had indeed found its way back to his body, he met with Wilbur and Lavinia for breakfast on the sun porch. True to their word, they furnished him with a copy of the purchase agreement to fax to his attorney.

Meanwhile, Sunny took a steaming bath that calmed her inner trembling. She then donned a pale blue sundress and took breakfast with Mrs. Lee and Malcolm in the kitchen. Knowing the value of input from employees who would be handling Saturday's reception, Sunny listened to their ideas, contributed a few of her own and thoroughly enjoyed muffins and coffee in the room where she had so often sat as a child, watching her grandmother cook. By the time breakfast was over, they'd decided on a menu to submit for Lavinia's approval.

Sunny then returned to the bedroom for her copy of the week's agenda. She'd have to reschedule activities postponed yesterday due to the media hoopla and Lavinia's sudden plans for Saturday. The trout-fishing contest, the tour of Asheville's historical mansions, the bicycling trip. As she studied the schedule, there was a knock at the bedroom door.

"Who is it?" She wanted to avoid reporters eager to ask questions or snap a photo. How long, she wondered, before some reporter exposed the truth—that Ryan and she were an unmarried, estranged couple sharing a bedroom? For monetary gain, no less. How tawdry it would sound.

A jovial, country voice replied, "Flowers for Mrs. Alexander."

Curious, Sunny opened the oak door a crack. There stood Grady Barrett with a bouquet of long-stemmed red roses.

"Grady! For heaven's sake—!"

Jonathon bounced merrily at his father's side. The boy immediately noticed the balcony and dashed for it. "Can I see our house from here?"

"You're welcome to try," Sunny invited with a fond smile, baffled by their presence. "Just don't climb over the railing," she warned.

"No, ma'am, I won't," he promised earnestly, pushing open the French doors and disappearing outside.

Grady handed Sunny a crystal vase of roses with his gallant, heart-stopping smile. "For you, sweet lady."

"They're beautiful." She inhaled their delicate fragrance. "But why for me?"

"Just my way of saying thank you for giving me a kick in the butt when I needed it. I wasn't thinking about Jonnie's feelings during that interview."

She grinned approvingly. "And I'm glad you're not angry with me. But you didn't have to bring flowers."

"You didn't have to speak up, either. If you hadn't, I might never have realized what I was doing to my best little buddy in the world." Grady's expression was openly affectionate. "Where's that old man of yours?"

"My—? Oh, you mean Ryan." Sunny set the crystal vase of roses on the oak dresser, the marriage masquerade weighing heavily on her mind. She felt uncomfortable lying to Grady. "He's meeting with Wilbur."

"Oh, yeah. Ryan mentioned something about buying Windsong Place. Hope it all goes through. Doesn't seem right, this place belonging to someone else."

"Would you like to sit on the balcony awhile?" she asked, feeling awkward in the bedroom with him.

"Nope, we can't stay. Jonnie and I are headed out to play some ball. But I was hoping you and Ryan could join us at my house for dinner tonight. We'll throw a few steaks on the grill, drink a few margaritas."

"And you can see my room," promised Jonathon with a bright smile on his freckled face.

"Sounds great. But I'll have to check with Ryan."

"Hey, Mrs. Alexander." Jonathon tugged on the full skirt of her sundress, and held up the smooth chunk of amethyst Ryan had given him. "This Pluto Power Crystal works!"

"It does?" Sunny asked, properly impressed.

"Sure." He polished it with his T-shirt, then gazed at it in awe. "I made a wish and it came true." He crooked his finger at Sunny, and she bent down so he could whisper in her ear. "Pa's gonna spend the whole week at home. With me!"

Delighted, Sunny laughed and gave him a thumbs-up.

"You'll make some lucky kid a great mom," remarked Grady, who'd been watching the scene. Sunny felt her cheeks warming beneath his admiring gaze. "Thanks again for setting me straight yesterday." He leaned forward and kissed her lightly on the lips.

Just then, the door swung open and Ryan walked in. Grady grinned. "There you are, old buddy. Caught me kissing your woman, didn't you? That'll teach you to leave your pretty little bride all alone. I just might steal her away."

"She'd turn your hair gray in a week, you dog," muttered Ryan as he sauntered past them.

His amiable reaction disappointed Sunny. It hadn't bothered him at all to walk in on Grady's kiss. And why should it? It had been meant in an innocent way, and besides, she was nothing to Ryan but a . . . A what? An employee? A bed partner? A casual roll in the hay?

"She'd be worth a whole head of gray hair," Grady replied with another glance at her. She was surprised to see a wistful glint in his blue eyes.

"How about dinner, my place, tonight?" Grady said, and belatedly, he shifted his gaze to Ryan. "You and Sunny."

"Thanks, Grady, but we can't." Ryan's gaze flickered to Sunny. "We're on our way to Asheville."

"Asheville?" she echoed. "Why?"

"Business."

"How about Thursday night, then?" Grady persisted. "Dinner at my house—and I won't take no for an answer."

Ryan nodded acceptance, then looked down at a sudden tugging at his shirt. "Hey, Mr. Alexander," Jonathon said, "thanks for the Pluto Power Crystal. It really works!"

"Told you." Ryan smiled and listened to the boy's excited chatter. After a few minutes, Grady and Jonathon took their leave. Locking the door behind them, Ryan turned to Sunny. "Pack an overnight bag."

"I can't go anywhere," she protested. "I've got to help Lavinia with preparations for the ceremony."

"That's what we'll be doing," he replied curtly, "preparing for the ceremony." He glanced at the expensive gold watch that gleamed on his suntanned wrist. "We have to leave now. You have identification with you, right? Your driver's license?"

Mystified, Sunny nodded.

"Good." Ryan's glance fell on the bouquet of roses in the crystal vase. He plucked the card from its holder. "Grady brought you roses?"

"Yes. Wasn't that sweet?"

With a short laugh that sounded more like a snort, Ryan muttered, "Nothing Grady does is ever sweet." Tossing the card down beside the bouquet, he scooped up his briefcase. "I'll go tell the Tanners we'll be back tomorrow night."

Sunny packed a suitcase while foreboding mushroomed within her. Some of her anxiety was caused by this sudden, unexplained change in plans, but mostly it stemmed from the energy that was radiating between Ryan and her.

What in heaven's name had she started?

As THEY HEADED SOUTH on the Blue Ridge Parkway in Ryan's low-riding black sports car, he handed Sunny a legal-looking document. The purchase agreement.

"Look at the signature section," he directed.

She did. "They want my signature, too?"

"Not only your signature. They want half the business in your name."

"Uh-oh. Can't we just tell them I prefer otherwise?"

"Lavinia won't hear of it. Something about the sisterhood of women, a wife's God-given right, and some lesson she learned at their Orlando location."

"I'll talk to her."

"No, you won't. Wilbur was a little too impressed by our rival bidder last night. Kept saying what a great guy he was. I have a feeling we'd better wrap up this deal now, before my father finds a way to discredit us."

They exchanged a contemplative glance. Sunny honestly wasn't sure how far Edgar would go to get what he wanted. He had opposed their original marriage with pit-bull ferocity, because it had ruined his plans for Ryan's future. The need for absolute control was almost a sickness with Edgar Rockwell Alexander, especially where his son was concerned. Had he mellowed over the years? Sunny doubted it.

"But I can't sign the purchase agreement as your wife," she pointed out. "That would be fraud, wouldn't it?"

"Too damned close to it for comfort. We're skating close enough to fraud already, introducing ourselves as husband and wife on national television. Renewing vows that were legally dissolved a long time ago. I never meant for the whole damned thing to get out of hand like it has."

"You're not going to give up Windsong Place, are you?"

"Hell, no. I mean to have my home back." Determination underscored his words. "There's just a few legalities we'll have to take care of before we sign this agreement."

"Before *we* sign?"

"We," he confirmed softly.

Sunny frowned a question.

Ryan smiled then—an odd, crooked smile that didn't quite warm his eyes. "We'll just have to get married again."

10

HIS PROPOSAL—if it could be called one—stunned Sunny.

Ryan interpreted her lack of reaction as acceptance. "I told Lavinia I'd hire the preacher for the, er, renewal of our vows. Only the preacher, you and I will know that a little legal paperwork preceded the ceremony."

"Paperwork!" she finally managed to say. "That's what you consider marriage—a little legal paperwork?"

He drew his brows together in a slight frown. "It wouldn't be a real marriage. Legal, maybe, but not binding. After our business transaction has been completed, and when the media loses interest, we'll . . . uh . . ."

She finished the sentence for him. "Divorce?"

With his gaze steady on the road ahead of them, he nodded. And repeated quietly, "Divorce."

The word sent a chill through her. "No," she whispered. "I can't do it."

"Of course you can." After a pause, he uttered dryly, "It's nothing you haven't done before."

Her breath caught in her throat. Yes, she had divorced him before. "Stop the car," she uttered.

"What?"

"I said, stop the car."

With one look at her—the first direct look he had given her all morning—Ryan slowed the car and swerved onto the grassy shoulder of the narrow mountain highway. Sunny sprang from the automobile and walked briskly away from it.

She stopped at the edge of the road, which overlooked a densely forested valley. The wind whipped her blond tendrils wildly around her face, and the skirt of her sundress billowed around her legs.

She told herself to breathe. In, then out. In, then out. Surely the function would become automatic again, in time. But would the terrible squeezing around her heart ever let up, and would the lump in her throat ever dissolve?

He'd sounded so casual about the whole thing. A little legal paperwork. And then, a divorce. Nothing they haven't done before.

The bastard! It hadn't been traumatic for him, it had just been the end of an ordeal. The vows they had taken—those empty, broken vows—had been nothing more than legalities necessary for the good of their unborn baby's future. They'd had nothing whatsoever to do with love.

She'd always known that, though, so why did it hurt all over again?

Standing there staring down into smoky treetops and russet slopes, Sunny hated Ryan. Hated him. Because he had not been touched, while she had been torn apart.

And nothing had changed. He'd been unaffected by their sexually explosive loving, while she felt as if she'd been reborn. She warned herself, *keep those defenses strong.*

When her breathing returned to a reasonable facsimile of normal, Sunny tossed a scathing glance over her shoulder to see him leaning against his gleaming black sports car, watching her.

"Something wrong?" he asked curtly.

"No. Nothing at all." The mountain wind whistled bleakly between them.

"Then let's go. We'll need blood tests and a license."

"Why the hell should I do this?" she cried, rounding on him, her hands balled into fists. "What's in it for me? I've never had to marry anyone before to get a management position. Somehow that's never been part of the job description."

"Do you think I like the idea any more than you do?" His dark scowl and curled lip stabbed her like a knife. "What started out as a personal matter has snowballed into a public one. *And* a legal one. If we don't marry, we'll be guilty of fraud."

"You get a million-dollar piece of property out of the deal. What do I get? To work for you? No picnic, I can promise you that."

He glowered at her for a moment, then conceded, "So I'll sweeten the pot."

Surprise silenced her, then she scoffed, "How?" He murmured something unintelligible. "What?"

Clearing his throat, he repeated, "I'll make you my partner."

She gaped at him. "What?"

"My partner," he repeated again, his voice heavy with reluctance. "I'll give you a percentage of ownership."

Sunny stared at him. "A percentage of Windsong Place?" It took a moment for the idea to sink in. She would *own* part of it. Forever. It would mean permanent job security. And a home—the home she had always loved. Wouldn't that meet all the goals she had set for herself? Wasn't he offering a solution to all of her problems? In a state very close to shock, she asked, "How much of a percentage?"

Ryan smiled wryly. "We'll negotiate on the way."

"Negotiate, hell. Fifty-fifty."

"You've got to be kidding. Windsong Place has been in my family for generations. My great-great-grandfather built it! Eighty-twenty is more like it."

"It doesn't matter who built it. You don't own it now." She sauntered toward the car. "Fifty-fifty, or nothing."

"Seventy-five, twenty-five. Take it or leave it."

"I'd leave it. You're lucky I didn't take you to the cleaners the last time we divorced. You're getting off easy this time around. Fifty-five, forty-five . . . that's my final offer."

SUNNY MOVED THROUGH each step of the premarital process in a daze. She avoided thinking about the end result of this day's work; something told her it would be counterproductive to do so. By one o'clock, they had finished with the blood tests and licensing paperwork, and arranged for a minister.

After lunching at an outdoor café with umbrella-shaded tables in downtown Asheville, they did not drive back to Windsong Place, which would have taken less than two hours. Nor did they check into a local hotel. Instead, Ryan took her to a private airport on the outskirts of Asheville, where they were met by his corporate jet.

"Where are we going?" inquired Sunny, wide-eyed.

"New York."

"New York! For what?"

Ryan smiled tightly as he guided her from his sports car to where the small jet thrummed, its uniformed pilot poised at the door in readiness. He yelled above the roar of the engine as they neared the craft, "You'll see."

Sunny preceded him up the few steps to the elegant interior. When they were seated comfortably inside, with the heavy door locked and their seat belts fastened, Sunny asked, "Are we going to New York for business?"

"I suppose you might call it that."

She gave up for a while. They lounged in plush, comfortable recliners, listened to relaxing music and sipped chilled Chablis. After watching the cottonlike clouds drifting below them, she finally turned to Ryan with another question. "To talk to your attorneys about the purchase?"

"No. My attorneys are in Philadelphia."

"To visit your New York office?"

"I might stop in."

His noncommittal answers only heightened her curiosity.

When she showed no sign of letting the subject drop, he shook his head with sardonic amusement. "Actually, I thought you could shop for a wedding gown."

For the second time that day, she was flabbergasted. "A wedding gown! Surely we don't have to buy a gown for this . . . this charade." The idea of donning real wedding apparel somehow made the ceremony even more of a mockery.

"The media's invited." His mouth twisted in a rueful imitation of a smile. "As Lavinia would say, think PR."

"I . . . I can't afford a wedding gown."

"It's just another business expense." His dry response, though lightly spoken, contained an element of harshness. He flipped open his wallet and tossed her a credit card.

Just another business expense, was it? If *that's* what he considered it . . .

Sunny spent that afternoon shopping with a vengeance. A limousine drove them to New York City's most exclusive shops and boutiques. At first, Ryan personally inspected each gown she tried on, deliberating over them as if the fate of his corporation depended on it, but after the first hour, he threw his hands up and sent Sunny off on her own. He retreated to the relative peace of his office.

For the first time in her life, Sunny set aside her natural tendency toward moderation. Just another business expense, huh? With blatant disregard for price, she indulged in what her grandmother would have called "pure choosiness."

She ended up buying a gown of ivory mirror taffeta, elegant in its simplicity and perfect for a garden ceremony. She also purchased ivory lingerie, pearl-beaded shoes, pearl-drop jewelry and other accessories she deemed necessary for "PR."

She was hoping that the cost of her shopping spree would make Ryan squirm, but later, when he took her to an extravagant restaurant for dinner, and then to his expensive Manhattan apartment, Sunny realized that the sum she had spent wouldn't cause him to blink an eye. He lived a life of consummate luxury.

Her role was dramatically clear. He was wining and dining her as he would any other woman with whom he was carrying on an affair. The international tycoon with his newest playmate. A business associate, of course. How chic.

She had only herself to blame. She had set the tone by insisting she was mature enough to handle a casual affair. And so she would be, she vowed. With iron determination, and a secret penchant for extravagance that she hadn't known she possessed, she played the game. And actually enjoyed it.

But then, the partying was over, and they were alone. Cinderella's clock struck midnight. All pretense dropped away. The urgency between them returned, and they made slow, needful love.

HIS CHANCE VISIT to the New York office got Ryan embroiled in personnel problems that required his attention the next morning, a drizzly gray Wednesday. Reluctantly, he sent Sunny back to Asheville ahead of him on a commercial flight; he didn't make his own escape until the next evening.

As he approached Windsong Place Thursday evening, he drank in the splendor of the many-gabled mansion and the lush surrounding gardens.

And remembered that it would never be exclusively his.

He had offered Sunny a percentage on impulse. Not his usual method of conducting business, but now that it was done, he felt he'd made the right decision.

Sunny belonged at Windsong Place. His feelings for the house were so strongly intertwined with memories of her that he couldn't entirely separate the two. She would live here, at his home. *Her* home.

He knew she wouldn't willingly leave it. Ever.

He parked his sports car in the circular front drive, wondering where he'd find her. He hadn't seen her since yesterday morning, when they'd made love in the shower. He leaned his head back against the leather headrest and allowed thoughts of her to wash over him in warm waves. She was a fever in his blood. A sweet, addictive fever. A fever that made the hours spent without her seem too long, and entirely pointless.

She'd be his again tonight.

His blood sang in sultry anticipation as he ascended the Grand Staircase, hoping to find her in their room. Instead, he found a note reminding him of dinner at Grady's. Grady, it seemed, had sent a car for Sunny. Ryan cursed in mild irritation. He wanted her here, with him, now.

He showered and changed from his business suit into a black shirt, fawn-colored jacket and jeans. Before leaving the house, he made a detour up the back hallway to the attic. He wanted to check on supplies he'd ordered, which should have been delivered to the attic while he was away.

The narrow stairway had been barely used in the past twenty-four years, since his mother's death. She had used the wooden-floored attic as her music room. At the top of the dim stairway, Ryan pushed open the solid oak door and peered inside. The place had been dusted and cleaned. Crates and boxes had been piled to one side, along with the few pieces of furniture he had ordered. So far, so good.

Satisfied, Ryan left and drove to Grady's three-story chalet that overlooked a scenic bend in the French Broad River.

Dinner, of course, was long over. A fire crackled in the grate. The lights were dimmed to a mellow glow. Grady, with his golden hair glinting in the firelight and his famous smile flashing, strummed his guitar and crooned a love song.

To Sunny.

She was seated across from him on the sofa, wearing a knit sweater dress of soft coral, holding a frosty margarita, looking starry-eyed as she watched Grady.

Since when had they become so damned chummy?

Noticing Ryan's presence, Grady stopped in the middle of the song and ribbed him about his lack of punctuality. Then thanked him for it, which was worse. Ryan pleasantly told him to go to hell.

Sunny didn't greet Ryan in any way—by word or deed. She merely lifted her eyes, slowly and cautiously, as if half fearing the contact with him. Ryan willed the contact. Insisted on it. But when she complied, electricity arced between them and left no room for small talk, no room for thought.

"Have a seat, old buddy," Grady said.

Ryan realized he'd been staring at Sunny—and she at him—for too long. And that he had missed her far too much in the two days they'd been apart. He took a seat on the sofa beside her, needing her nearness, but he directed his attention to Grady. "Where's Jonathon?"

"Asleep, I hope." Grady set aside his pearl-handled acoustic guitar. "Sunny tucked him in about an hour ago."

"He sleeps with his Pluto Crystal under his pillow," she said, a flush of pleasure rising in her cheeks. Her lips curved into a smile that went to Ryan's head like whiskey.

Unable to resist the impulse to touch her, he swept his hand across her slender back, then rested his arm behind her on the back of the sofa. A deliberately possessive pose. As if he needed to establish his claim on her. Ridiculous, he knew. But his arm remained where it was, all the same.

Grady poured Ryan a Scotch and recounted comic mischief they had shared as kids, which evolved into a hearty exchange of blame and good-natured insults. Sunny laughed and threw in a few jibes of her own.

Ryan realized there was no reason for tension, and he scorned his earlier reaction. He was among friends.

"Hope your purchase of the house goes through," Grady said, refilling Sunny's glass from a frosty silver shaker. "It'll be good to have you two next door again. Like old times."

Ryan swirled the ice around in his glass of Scotch. "I hear you don't spend much time up here, anyway."

"That's about to change." Grady smiled at Sunny. "I've seen the error of my ways. Need to spend more time at home, with my boy. Sunny tells me you're going to be on the road quite a bit yourself," he added, a little too casually.

Ryan's tension returned tenfold. What would happen when their marriage masquerade was over, and Sunny was managing the inn? Grady would be here, the charming next-door neighbor, in need of a mother for Jonnie.

He himself would be hundreds of miles away.

Grady pulled his guitar back into his lap. "Lemme play you another song," he drawled softly.

As Grady strummed, a thought hit Ryan squarely in the gut. Sunny's next goal was to find a husband, one foolish enough to believe in forever or ruthless enough to let *her* believe so.

He inspected Grady with a new, critical eye. She wanted someone who shared her views. Grady would say whatever she wanted to hear. Successful, she'd said. Grady certainly was that. She'd mentioned good-looking. Grady was a woman-pleaser, all right. A sense of humor? Always. Good with kids? Grady was already working on it.

What if she fell for it? Ryan's heart gave a sickening thud. He clenched his jaw. He was ready to leave, ready to take Sunny home to bed.

"Time to go, Sunny," he said, his voice hoarse and gruff. Her eyes darkened in a familiar way, arousing him as always.

"You go on back home, old buddy," Grady said. "I'll bring Sunny later. She still has to choose a song for after the ceremony."

A wild possessiveness ripped through Ryan. "I think it's time for all of us to call it a night."

Sunny promptly rose and headed for Jonnie's room. "I promised to say goodbye to him if he's still awake. I'd better go check."

As she disappeared down the long corridor, Grady murmured, "That Sunny. She's one heck of a woman. If she wasn't your wife, Alexander, I'd steal her away from you." He flashed his famous smile.

Anxiety twisted Ryan's gut. In a very short time, Sunny wouldn't be his wife. "You touch her and I'll kill you."

Grady sat back down, crossed his arms behind his head and grinned up at Ryan. "Know what I'm gonna do? I'm gonna buy Sunny a wedding gift. Something she'd really like. But what?"

The kind of inspiration that strikes only once, maybe twice, in a lifetime, embraced Ryan at that moment. "I can think of one thing she's always wanted. But—" he paused for maximum effect "—it's expensive."

Grady waved away paltry obstacles. "Money's no object. What should I get her?"

Ryan gravely replied, "A mink coat."

HE PARKED HIS CAR on the moonlit lot behind Windsong Place, where their grassy ball field had once been. Together Sunny and he walked across the blacktop. To their left, directly behind the house, was the courtyard and rose garden that surrounded the gazebo, where they would soon be married.

Sunny noticed the direction of his gaze. "Lavinia's planning to decorate outside tomorrow. We'll set chairs over there to form a central aisle. The minister will stand on the gazebo. You and I—" her voice grew quiet and strained "—will walk up the aisle. Together. Lavinia feels that since we're, uh, already married, it would be more symbolic than meeting at the front."

Ryan did not reply. He realized what had been weighing so heavily on his mind tonight wasn't the threat of Grady. He understood that now, as he pictured Saturday's ceremony, and what would happen afterward. The cake would be cut, toasts would be made, photos would be taken. The bride and groom would make their escape. But not together.

No honeymoon would follow. No wedding night. They'd sign the purchase agreement, then carry on with their respective lives. She, at Windsong Place. He, anywhere but.

The simple problem was he didn't want to leave her.

They reached the redbrick walkway lined with shrubbery and blossoming flowers, and Ryan laced his fingers through hers and led her through the courtyard.

Sunny glanced up at him, surprised that he hadn't guided her directly to their room. His touch, his stare, his hurry to leave, all had communicated his desire as clearly as a passionate kiss. And she, God help her, returned that desire. Every time they made love, though, she lost a little more of her confidence in her ability to walk away.

And she would need that ability, very soon.

They strolled through the dim, rose-scented courtyard accompanied by the distant music of the rushing river and gently chirping crickets. She wanted to forget their inevitable parting. She wanted to forget the way she had missed him so desperately when they'd been apart for less than two days. She wanted to enjoy the magic of being with him. Savor it. Store it somewhere deep in her memory.

With no explanation, Ryan led her around the far side of the mansion, to the service entrance at the back.

"Where are we going?"

He replied with a mysterious smile.

"Uh-oh. Last time you surprised me, we ended up in New York City." They climbed the dimly lit back stairway to the attic and her curiosity heightened. Ryan opened the door and touched a switch on the wall. Bright light flooded the massive attic.

The place had been dusted and polished. The octagonal windows, which lined the walls beneath the sloping ceiling, sparkled. And in the center of the floor had been placed an easel, a drawing table, unopened packs of canvas, a drying rack and a small electric jewelry kiln. Equipment she once would have killed for. Sunny stared.

He had amassed everything necessary for an art studio!

Hands in his jacket pockets, Ryan paced the vast room, his footsteps echoing. "Plenty of sun in both morning and afternoon," he pointed out, glancing toward the windows. "And on that wall, you can display your paintings. You know...show them." He stopped, and without looking at her, asked quietly, "Think inspiration might strike here?"

Gazing around in awed surprise, she murmured, "This is for me?"

"Just an idea." He sounded embarrassed. "So Madam Innkeeper doesn't forget about that starving artist inside her."

A profound tenderness welled up and pushed at the inner walls of her chest. She turned around in a slow circle, imagining the possibilities. "Oh, Ry...it's perfect."

He watched her in silent pleasure. She danced over to him and hugged him. His eyes darkened, his arms closed around her and he pulled her closer. The hug quickly turned into something more, something desperate and swaying.

"Sunny." His husky whisper was like the heady fragrance of roses. "When you took this job, I agreed to leave you here to manage the inn alone." He gazed down at her with heart-stopping hunger. "But I can't stay away."

Sunny caught her breath. Questions rushed to her tongue, but sudden hope made her too vulnerable to ask them. She finally managed to whisper, "Are you...talking about living here?"

"I can. I thought I might set up an office here. Get back in the swing of programming some of my own software."

Her heartbeat had slowed. "How long would you stay?"

"Days, maybe weeks . . ." The expression on her face, or perhaps her lack of response, prompted him to add, "You won't have to change any of your plans."

Suddenly, she understood. All too well. She broke away from his embrace.

"Sunny?"

She couldn't speak. Couldn't find words. She ran for the door, and her steps clattered on the stairway. It was as if Windsong's ghost was chasing her.

RYAN WAS STUNNED. What in the hell had her reaction meant? Didn't she want him to come back to Windsong Place after the purchase had been finalized? Didn't she want him? He knew she did. Sunny wasn't the kind of woman who could make love with such tenderness and passion if she didn't truly want him.

So then why hadn't she been happy at his change in plans?

After walking around the moonlit grounds, weary from the questions clambering inside his head, Ryan wandered past the porte cochere with its gleaming carriage and stopped at the rocker-lined front porch. Staring at the glossy oak door, he gave in to a sudden, overpowering urge to turn around.

He found himself gazing out at the sloping front drive. He was looking for a car—a sleek, gray sedan. He wished fervently for its approach.

The car did not materialize.

Of course not. Ryan shook his head to dispel the odd fancy. What had made him think of such a car pulling up in the drive? And why, as he stood alone on the porch gazing bleakly into the darkness, did sadness overwhelm him? Sadness, and a deep, hollow ache?

He turned abruptly away from the sight of the front drive and entered the dimly lit Oak Hall. Whatever had caused the hollow feeling, he knew only one thing for certain: he had felt it many times before.

Most recently when he had watched Sunny gazing starry-eyed into Grady's smiling face.

There was only one way Ryan knew how to make the ache go away. His footsteps quickened as he climbed the Grand Staircase to the bedroom where Sunny would be waiting. He hoped.

11

SHE STOOD NEAR the open French doors and allowed the bracing night wind to comb through her hair, not caring that it chilled her to the marrow. She couldn't hide from the truth anymore. She loved him. With her whole heart and soul, she loved him. She wanted him to stay with her, not only for sporadic visits, but for the rest of their lives.

But Ryan didn't believe in lifetime guarantees. And he didn't believe in love. As soon as he felt the threat of "emotional dependence," as he called it, his walls would spring up, shutting her out.

History was repeating itself. They had indulged freely, foolishly, in physical passion, building a need for each other that superseded all logic. Tomorrow, they would marry for a practical purpose. Again. And soon, she'd divorce him, with his full approval. Again.

But this time, as manager and co-owner of the inn, she wouldn't be able to protect what was left of her heart by running away. And Ryan could live here whenever he chose. With whomever he chose. She would be trapped here, managing the inn, pretending she wasn't dying inside.

A key jiggled in the lock. Sunny didn't turn around. The door opened, and after a moment, she heard his hoarse whisper. "Why did you run from me, Sunny?"

Facing the open French doors and the blinding night breeze, she whispered, "Because I was wrong, Ry. I prom-

ised that sex between us wouldn't lead to complications."
She turned and met his frown. "But it has."

He sat on the bed, leaned back against the headboard
and crossed his muscled forearms over his chest. His look
commanded her to explain.

"I realize you've given me everything I've asked for—a
job, a home, a good salary, an excellent benefit package.
A secure f-future." Her vision blurred with unshed tears.
"Your body, your time."

"But it's not enough," he stated flatly.

She shook her head. "No. It's not enough."

Anger burned in his smoke-gray eyes. He made no move
toward her, but his next words exploded with quiet passion. "Damn it, Sunny, what the hell do you want from
me?"

"You," she replied. "I want you."

His gaze didn't soften. "You have me."

"For how long? Until the time comes when you don't
want me in your life?"

Never, thought Ryan. He'd never stop wanting her. The
truth of that shook him. He wanted her with him—in his
home, in his bed—indefinitely. He wanted to possess her
entirely.

Warning bells went off in his head. She was getting too
necessary. Too important. Too close. With the warning
came the sick, cold feeling of dread.

"I want your love," Sunny whispered, pleading with
him. "I want you to love me. Because I love you."

For one unguarded moment, his eyes burned into hers
as if he were gazing at a prize he could never claim; a paradise he would never enter. But in the next second, those
eyes became shuttered and dark.

Sunny saw the door slam shut, sensed his absolute
withdrawal.

"You want words?" he taunted. "Pretty words?" He shook his head. "No. I won't lie to you that way, Sunny. I don't understand why you'd want me to." In quiet fury, he left the bed and strode past her. "We'll stick to our original agreement. You manage the inn. I'll be an absentee owner—" he cast a glance over his shoulder, his gaze connecting with hers "—and leave you the hell alone."

He disappeared into the dressing room and slammed the bathroom door.

Sunny closed her eyes as a wave of anguish washed over her. The walls around his heart were insurmountable, at least to her.

In cold misery, she wandered out onto the balcony to stare into the night.

She remained outside until he had settled down on the cot. It seemed an eternity until the rhythmic sound of his breathing convinced her he was asleep.

She packed in the dark.

Hurting, bleeding as if she were amputating her own arms and legs, she penned him a note, then slipped the borrowed wedding band off her finger.

RYAN WOKE SHORTLY before sunrise and noticed that Sunny had already risen. And made the bed. Ever efficient.

His anger of the previous night returned full force, and he clenched his teeth as he stalked into the bathroom for a shower. He wanted it stingingly cold, bitterly, and he welcomed the numbness that overtook him.

He shaved as if it were a normal day, as if the old emptiness weren't pressing in around him, like wolves stalking him in the wilderness. But he noticed her toothbrush was missing from beside his. Her shampoo and toiletries were gone.

Wrapping a towel around his waist, he stepped out of the bathroom and saw that the dressing area held none of her belongings. Her clothing and her suitcases were gone. His apprehension grew as he pushed through the bedroom door.

Nothing of her remained.

A glinting object on the dresser caught his eye. The gold wedding band. Beside it, a note. A terrible heaviness settled into his chest as he scanned the familiar writing.

I want you to be happy, Ry. You won't be if you live without love. If you can't love me, go find your Mrs. Right. And hire another manager for the inn. I can no longer consider living here. Tell Lavinia and Wilbur anything you like.

S.

Ryan stared at the note in stunned disbelief. It made no sense. None. How could she say she wanted him to be happy, yet tell him to find someone else? He couldn't do both.

And what did she mean by "find your Mrs. Right," as if he would possibly consider marrying anyone other than her? She was the only one to whom he would ever give his name. Only she brought the laughter and the pleasure and the gut-level thrills he craved. She also brought the anger, and sometimes the rage. No one else had the right. No one else had the power. Only Sunny.

She made him feel. She made him see and taste.

She made him love.

Ryan sank down on the bed, staring straight through the paper in his hands. The revelation blinded him. He loved her. He loved her so fiercely that if she had truly left him . . . if he had to live without her again . . .

Like a fuse blowing beneath a power surge, darkness suddenly engulfed him. The deep, nameless dread was back. He lowered his head, his forearms pressing against his knees.

He wasn't sure how much time passed before he struggled to his feet, and he dressed in a daze. *Love brings the pain.* When had he learned that? He couldn't recall the circumstances, but he acutely remembered the result. Bitter, paralyzing pain.

He wouldn't fall victim to it again. He was strong enough to avoid it this time. He had lived without Sunny for ten long years. He could damn sure live without her again.

He simply could not tolerate needing anyone as much as he needed Sunny.

LATER THAT DAY, Ryan informed Wilbur and Lavinia saying he no longer intended to buy Windsong Place. He wanted to be gone. Every room, every corner, vibrated with images of Sunny.

Emptiness squeezed him breathless.

Jamming his hands into his pockets, he headed for his room to pack. But instead of his room, he somehow found himself in the vast, echoing attic that would have been Sunny's studio.

The late-afternoon sun was blotted out by clouds and failed to dispel its gloom. He walked past the crates of canvases, the drawing table, all the supplies he had foolishly ordered.

He'd been looking forward to watching her work, watching the light dance off her fingers as they evoked beauty, seeing her spirit soar. But she had left him.

Something pricked at a memory. The memory of pain he had forgotten. He had come to this attic when he was a boy. He had come here to listen to music. Piano music. He must have been very young, because his father had locked the attic long before Sunny had come into his life as a pesky little girl.

He remembered a woman playing, her fingers quick and graceful on the ivory-and-ebony keys as he sat on the bench beside her. The memory brought with it a strong, warm tenderness. And an odd resentment.

The woman had been his mother. He remembered that now.

As if magnetically drawn, he moved toward the front window and peered through the freshly polished glass. The sloping front drive of Windsong Place was spread out before him.

Without warning, another memory descended upon him, and suddenly the dimness of the attic was the bright warmth of a summer afternoon. He was on the front porch, beside a suitcase that was almost as big as he was.

His mother was calling his name. Gentle hands brushed his cheek. Slender, caring hands. He inhaled the comforting fragrance of her perfume, and another scent. Cinnamon, like the cookies she baked. She tucked one into his hand now, it was warm from the oven.

"Don't cry, angel." She wiped the tears from his cheek and kissed him. Her own eyes were red and puffy. "I'll come back for you when I get things worked out. I love you." She engulfed him in a hug.

He wanted to go with her but hands pulled him back. The large, rough hands of his father. He cried and fought, but his mother kept walking, suitcase in her hand. He could hear her crying—his mother crying!—as she tossed the suitcase into the back seat and slid behind the wheel of her shiny gray car.

His father growled, "She's not going to take you any-where." Then he stared after the car as it pulled away, his eyes hard and angry. "Nothing in this world will hurt you worse than the woman you love. Remember that, son."

Though he didn't know his father very well, Ryan knew his mother. She'd promised and she'd be back. She always kept her promises.

The brightness of the afternoon dimmed. The warmth cooled. Darkness descended. Still, he sat on the top step of the porch and waited, watching the front drive for her shiny gray car to return.

He had waited there the next day, too. And the next.

Remembering, Ryan gasped in the musty attic air as the pain of her betrayal seared through him. He had trusted her, but she had lied. She hadn't come back for him. Ever.

Frozen in front of the attic window, staring at the driveway, Ryan relived all the hurting, the grieving. The hating. Eventually, he had come to hate her.

How could he have forgotten all of this so completely?

He squeezed his eyes shut. He wanted to turn away from the movie running in his head, push it aside, make the hurting stop. Just when he thought he would explode, an inner voice whispered, *Look again. Look at the whole picture.*

Ryan stood very still, replaying his mother's betrayal one more time. Mysteriously, another piece of that long-ago day surfaced from the deepest murky recesses of his mind.

He hadn't simply waited on the porch for her return. He remembered that now. He had run down the garden steps and into the woods, as fast as his legs would carry him. If he took the shortcut, he could stop her on the road, just before the second curve. Branches and brambles tore at his clothes and scraped his face. Down the path he raced until he reached the paved highway.

But he was a moment too late. As he stepped onto the grassy shoulder of the road, the gray car whizzed by. Disappointment tore through him. Disappointment, and sudden fear.

He remembered the sharp squeal of tires around the curve, the crunch of metal, the shattering of glass. The splintering sound of the tree.

And he remembered the smell of burning rubber. The acrid taste of thick black smoke that scalded his eyes and throat as he searched for her. He saw her through the broken glass of the back window, her hair all wet with blood. . . .

She had died that day. Clarity struck Ryan like lightning. The pain seared through him again. But it was a different kind of burning this time. A cleansing one.

As though a blindfold had been ripped away, he opened his eyes. She hadn't deliberately left him. She hadn't betrayed him at all. Death had taken her.

Slowly, gradually, a gentle wave of understanding eased the tension from his rigid muscles and softened the sharp edges of his pain. Olive had explained to him about his mother's death, he remembered now. Olive had told him she was with the angels. But he'd refused to understand.

He had insisted on waiting for her.

Ryan tried to envision his mother, but the fragments wouldn't pull together. The tone of her voice and the color of her hair eluded him. Too many years had passed since he had sat beside her as she played her piano. Too many years since he had waited on the porch for her return. But he remembered her softness.

"This is why you drew me back to Windsong Place, isn't it?" he whispered. "To make our peace."

The wind mellowed into a soothing music. Ryan swore he could smell cinnamon cookies. He tucked her memory away, deep within his heart, for safekeeping.

Before he could savor his newfound peace, another thought intruded. The thought of luminous green eyes, silken hair, and a softness his soul craved. Sunny. *His* Sunny.

No. Not his.

Rain pelted the attic windows. Thunder rumbled with ancient fury and shook the very earth. Thunder. With it came a slender, wide-eyed woman pattering to his side, her image so vivid, Ryan reached out to touch her.

But as the thunder faded, so did the woman. Leaving only the mournful song of the wind. And the same old emptiness.

"GET UP, GAL."

Sunny squinted through one eye, then sat up in Olive's old-fashioned feather bed. "Grandma! What are you doing out of the hospital? They told me they'd release you tomorrow. You didn't steal the doctor's car again, did you?"

"I don't steal cars, I borrow 'em," Olive grumbled.

"I drove her" came a voice from the doorway. Cool and regal as ever, Lavinia Tanner stood in the bedroom doorway. "To help me look for you. I take it you and Ryan had a fight."

Shoving her sleep-mussed hair out of her eyes, Sunny wished it were as simple as a fight. Striving to retain some modicum of dignity, she replied, "We've reevaluated our relationship. Readjusted our goals. Revamped our agendas."

"A fight!" concluded Olive.

"But Sunny, dear, about tomorrow," said Lavinia. "We really *must* talk."

"You're darned tootin'," Olive muttered, squaring her jaw. "I told Lavinia here that no granddaughter of mine would run out on an obligation just because of man problems. Especially not when the whole gol-derned community's planning to show up."

"I don't understand you, Grandma. You raised a fuss a few days ago, saying that Ryan was going to break my heart. So why are you so determined to see us together now?"

"When you and Ryan dragged me into the parlor for tea, I saw how things were. Your heart's already broken, gal. Has been for years. I'm hoping that mule-headed boy I raised finds out he's got a heart somewhere, too. Otherwise, you can kiss yours goodbye."

"He has a heart," whispered Sunny. "I'm just not in it."

"Then doing the right thing by Lavinia tomorrow won't make matters any worse." The bulldog tenacity in Olive's green eyes told Sunny that arguing would be fruitless.

Instead, she turned to the thin-lipped woman beside her. "Lavinia," she implored, "please accept my apology, but I won't be running the inn. Ryan and I are—" she swallowed convulsively "—parting ways. The ceremony would be a lie."

"Such is the nature of PR work, dear," murmured Lavinia, unperturbed. "The media will lose interest soon enough. *After* the ceremony." She sat down on the bed and laid a gentle hand on Sunny's quilt-covered knee. "I wouldn't presume to interfere in your personal life, Sunny. But you've done a lovely job at the inn. In one week, you've won the devotion of the staff, and the guests are raving about the changes you've made. The inn comes alive when you and Ryan are there. Don't let a quarrel stand in the way of your future."

"I have no future with Ryan."

Lavinia and Olive both stared at her glumly.

"Then I'm asking as a friend," said Lavinia. "Won't you please go through with the ceremony? For my sake?" Looking self-conscious, Lavinia studied her gleaming red fingernails. "I've, uh, invited a few of Ryan's friends who called after seeing the televised interview. People from the very best, the very *oldest* families. These contacts could be beneficial for all of us. Wilbur and I *are* selling franchises for other Tanner Resort Inn locations, you know." Her gaze squarely pinned Sunny down. "Surely you won't leave me looking like a fool?"

Sunny was in big trouble. She had, after all, agreed to take part in the ceremony. She *had* been part of its planning. In all good conscience, she could not refuse to walk down that aisle tomorrow morning.

12

SATURDAY DAWNED BRIGHT and warm. The springtime fragrance of wildflowers, blossoming trees and grassy meadows scented the clear North Carolina mountain air. Windsong Place—every peak, every gable, every mullioned window— sparkled with a special luster.

It was a cruel joke of nature, thought Sunny, that today she would whisper her goodbyes and walk away from Windsong forever. And the day and the place were perfect for a wedding.

The ceremony was scheduled to begin at eleven. Olive cranked up her old Chevy and drove Sunny to Windsong Place early.

While Olive inspected the house she had worked in for forty-some years, Sunny went directly to Lavinia's suite, avoiding the hallway that led to Ryan's room. She didn't want to see him before the ceremony. If she had to risk facing him again, she preferred that it be in public, where private communication would be impossible.

To her relief, she learned he had spent the night away, and hadn't yet returned.

"He promised he'd be back in time," Lavinia fretted. She had been checking her watch at ten-minute intervals.

Sunny refused to contemplate where Ryan might be. She almost hoped he wouldn't show. She'd rather suffer the public humiliation of being a jilted bride than the private hell of seeing—and leaving—Ryan again.

THE GRANDFATHER CLOCK chimed as the hairdresser coaxed Sunny's curls into some kind of order and Lavinia announced that Ryan would be late.

"He called from his apartment in New York!" she declared perplexed. "He needed something from home, he said. What in heaven's name do you think it could be?"

Sunny didn't care to guess.

Lavinia continued, "He asked if I'd found his wallet. He lost it—it has quite a few credit cards in it."

"Lost his wallet?" repeated Olive. "Ain't like him. Some New York pickpocket got it, that's what."

Before Olive could launch into her diatribe about the evils of the big city, Sunny ducked into a vacant bedroom and pressed her back to the closed door, desperately trying to bolster her courage. Only a little longer, she promised herself, and the whole charade would be over.

OLIVE FOUND HER, and returned her to the hairdresser. Artfully he weaved a pearl-beaded tiara through her curls and attached the shoulder-length veil.

When she finally had a moment alone, Sunny stared in the mirror attached to the bedroom door. The gown of ivory taffeta shone with an elegant luster. Hand-beading detailed the fitted bodice and the lace-edged portrait neckline. Lovely though it was, Sunny knew the gown was nothing more than a costume. And she felt like a fraud.

"A smile might put a little color in your cheeks," Olive suggested, looking resplendent herself in a dress of pink chiffon. Sunny forced a smile. Olive's lips quirked downward. "Forget it. Try some rouge."

As the sound of voices from the garden grew into the dull murmuring of a crowd, Olive hurried out to greet her friends and neighbors from Heaven's Hollow.

The door swung shut behind her, then immediately opened again. Sunny's eyes rounded in surprise. "Fran!"

Her assistant manager sallied in with one slender, jeweled hand on her hip, her penciled brows raised in feigned arrogance. "So, you *do* remember my existence? Good thing, considering I drove half the night through mountains to attend a wedding to which I wasn't invited."

Fran's familiar foghorn voice brought a lump to Sunny's throat. An ally, at last! Someone to hold on to when the final goodbyes had been said. Someone to guide her back to Atlanta, force her to eat, to sleep, to breathe . . .

"Oh, Fran!" Sunny threw her arms around the petite brunette. "How did you even know . . . ?"

"Not from you! I had to find out about my best friend's wedding from Daphne, who saw something about it on television. Were my feelings hurt? Crushed, hon. I was crushed like a bug. Sure, I understand being swept off your feet by wild, reckless passion. It's one of my fondest aspirations. But I still can't believe that you would *marry anyone* without even—"

"I'm not marrying anybody, Fran."

"What?" Fran blinked her extraordinarily long lashes. "I hate to harp on details, hon, but this gorgeous ivory dress and those pearl-beaded shoes aren't exactly beachwear."

"The wedding's not real. It's a sham."

"A sham? Get outta here! You're about to marry Mr. Six-Foot-Three, Sexy-Gray-Eyes, Twenty-Million-Bucks-or-More. . . ." Catching sight of Sunny's face, Fran stopped. "Oh. Oh, no. Oh, hon." She put an arm around Sunny's shoulder, her voice drastically subdued. "Is it bad?"

"Bad." Sunny swiped at a tear with the back of her hand.

Fran opened her slim green silk purse, drew out a tissue and blotted the wetness from Sunny's cheek. "I have no idea what's going on, but we can always sue him for something. Breach of contract, maybe. I read about this bride who—"

"I'm not going to sue him, Fran." Sunny took the tissue and blew her nose. "I'm simply going to l-leave him."

Fran's eyes brimmed with concern. "You've been alone for as long as I've known you, and I never understood why." A sad smile curved her mouth. "Until I saw you with him." She squeezed Sunny's hands. "He's your other half."

Sunny stared at her through a blur. "No," she whispered. "I don't mean anything to him. I'm just another woman in a world full of them. When this farce is over, Fran, take me back to Atlanta."

Fran reluctantly released Sunny's hands. "If you say so."

Sunny glanced at her tear-smudged face in the mirror. "I can't go down there looking like this."

Fran glanced at her watch. "You still have twenty minutes. I don't think the groom's even here yet. But if you're not ready in time, I'll ask that Roman-type god with the country twang to play a few songs. He's even better-looking in person than he is on album covers. Daphne will be green. Pure green." Fran sashayed out of the room.

Sunny took a deep breath, collected herself, then repaired her makeup. As she applied mascara, the soft strains of music reached her ears.

Her heart contracted. Had the wedding march begun?

But then she realized it was not the wedding march. Nor was it coming from the garden. Puzzled, she set down her mascara wand and stole closer to the door.

It sounded like piano music.

And it was coming from the attic.

SHE FELT FOOLISH for coming up here. She stood alone in the middle of the huge, unfurnished room with sunlight slanting like slices of heaven through its many windows. There was no piano.

It must have been the sound of the mountain wind singing through the gables. The same eerie song that had kept her awake many nights when she had lived here as a child. The one that had sent her scurrying through lonely shadows to the warmth of Ryan's bed.

The song of the house's ghost.

Sunny turned to go back down, passing by the crates, boxes and art supplies that Ryan had bought for her. She refused to be touched by the memory. She could not allow herself to mistake his generosity, his obvious desire to please her, for love. He would never give his heart.

Her heels echoed on the wooden floorboards as she headed toward the door. The soft taffeta of her gown rustled. The toe of her beaded ivory shoe hit into something small and soft, sent it whispering across the floor.

A wallet. A man's black eelskin wallet glinted in the pool of sunlight. Sunny bent down and retrieved it. Lavinia had mentioned something about Ryan losing his wallet.

Slowly she rose to her feet and opened the slim billfold. On one side, she found credit cards. On the other side, Ryan's New York driver's license.

She knew she shouldn't look further, but curiosity overpowered her. With only a token pang of guilt, she leafed through its contents. What she was looking for, she wasn't sure. A clue, she supposed, to the real Ryan. To what kind of things he carried around with him, day in and day out.

The first thing she found was cash—tens, twenties and fifties. Insurance cards. Business cards. But nothing personal. No photos, no scribbled phone numbers, no theater stubs, no souvenirs. All business. Strictly business.

It occurred to her then that she really didn't know him. After all they'd been to each other, she couldn't swear he cared too deeply about anybody, or anything.

Sadness wrung her heart.

Her throat constricted, and she wished in a fervent prayer that someone, someday, would tap that hidden reservoir of love she instinctively knew he carried within him.

As she folded the wallet closed, one tiny corner stuck up awkwardly. A business card, probably, dislodged from its place. She reopened the wallet and realized it wasn't a business card. She grasped the protruding corner and pulled.

It was a photograph. Old, somewhat yellowed, with dog-eared corners and tiny creases. A photograph, taken many years ago, of a girl in a white sundress. She was wearing a single strand of pearls, and orange blossoms in her hair.

"HE'S HERE. Your groom has arrived," Lavinia announced, watching Sunny descend the stairway from the attic. "Are you okay, dear?" With a quick, nervous glance up the stairway, she murmured, "You look like you've seen a ghost."

Sunny barely heard her. In her heart, hope warred with wisdom. The old photograph that he'd kept behind his license had been only that—a photograph. She couldn't read too much into that . . . could she?

"You're just having last-minute jitters. Every bride has them." Lavinia stuck a cool, fragrant bouquet into Sunny's hand and firmly wrapped her fingers around the stem. "You look lovely, dear. Breathe deeply. Keep your chin up.

Ah, there's the prelude to the wedding march. That's your cue."

The beckoning melody sent quivers of apprehension through Sunny. If Lavinia hadn't been at her side, firmly sweeping her along the corridor toward the back door, she would have bolted in the opposite direction.

"Enter from between the rose trellises," instructed Lavinia. "Ryan will be waiting there on your right."

Holding the bouquet against her as a warrior might hold a shield, Sunny preceded Lavinia outside into the red-bricked courtyard, hidden from the view of the seated guests by immense trellises covered in white and yellow roses.

Ryan was not waiting where Lavinia had told her he would be. Instead, he stood inside the rose arbor, out of the spectators' view. He looked calm, sophisticated and utterly debonair in a tuxedo of dark gray that fit his broad-shouldered form to tailored perfection. His jet hair gleamed with elegance, and the strong, angled planes of his sun-bronzed face had never looked more handsome.

But it was his eyes, silvery and hypnotic, that embraced her the moment she stepped outside.

Her heart rose to her throat as she approached him. She saw his awed gaze absorbing her—her gown, her face, the flowers woven through her hair. And when his eyes at last met hers, the message they conveyed kindled a longing in her.

He thought her beautiful.

It was not the first time he had looked at her with such an intensely masculine perusal. But it always felt like the first time. Without breaking eye contact, he offered his arm.

She placed her hand there and felt the forceful tension in the muscles beneath his jacket sleeve.

"Sunny," he said, his warm breath stirring her hair. "The cameras, the people—they don't mean a damned thing."

Her lips parted, but she didn't reply. He was right. Nothing mattered, excepting holding to the truths she had learned over the course of her heartbreak. Not an easy task, while thrilling beneath the power of his stare.

Behind them, Lavinia gasped and whispered furiously, "The cameras and people *do* matter! Sunny, hold your bouquet lower. Remember *to walk slowly,* together. Hesitate, step. Hesitate, step. And keep your eyes straight ahead, on the minister." She gave them both a push to get them started.

They stepped together into the opening of the rose-covered archway. The music changed from the light prelude of the wedding march to the deep, blood-stirring chords of "Here Comes the Bride."

Rows of seated guests turned toward them with admiring stares, nods, murmurs, smiles. Lined with a white runner and strewn with rose petals, the aisle looked interminably long. At the end were two stairs leading up to the flower-bedecked gazebo, where a lanky, bespectacled minister clad in flowing white robes waited with a benign smile. From the corner of her eye, Sunny caught sight of cameras.

"I want you to know, Sunny," Ryan whispered into her ear as they took the first graceful hesitate-step down the aisle. "I've never believed in the mercenary killing of mink."

She glanced at him in surprise, unsure she had heard him correctly. But it was time to take the second hesitate-step, and Lavinia had told her to keep her eyes straight ahead. Determined to do things right, she hesitated, then stepped. In perfect unison with her groom.

Leaning closer to her this time, he whispered, "And I am fairly successful in my career." His statement was almost lost beneath the ever-swelling music. "You can call my accountant and verify my funds."

Urged on by the eyes of the crowd, they took another hesitate-step.

"Funds?" she whispered, looking at Ryan instead of the minister. "I don't care about your funds."

"Step," he said.

"Step?"

"Now."

Missing only a fraction of the "hesitate," Sunny stepped.

"And usually, I manage to keep a sense of humor. Okay, sometimes it wears a little thin," he admitted.

She frowned at him. Then hesitated, and stepped.

From the side of his mouth, he continued, "You might not believe this, but I do like kids."

Hesitate-step.

"And if you don't like my looks, there's always plastic surgery."

She completely forgot to step that time. But so did he. They made it up the moment they realized it, maintaining some semblance of unison.

"Don't you dare change a thing!" she admonished him.

They had reached the two stairs leading to the gazebo. Ryan turned her to face him.

"I know I'm not missing that last requirement on your list, Sunny," he breathed. "If you say I am, you're lying. Our lovemaking is—" He shook his head, searching for words. With darkening eyes, he whispered, "Heaven."

Together they slipped into a gaze, each straining to read the other's thoughts, each struggling to find clarity.

The music, which had reached its crescendo, backed off and started over. Somewhere above them, a man cleared his throat. The crowd behind them murmured.

"None of those requirements matter," she said. "Thank you for teaching me that. I hope someday you learn what *is* important." She tried to turn away, to continue their march.

But Ryan refused to release her gracefully. He knew if he let her go this time, she'd be lost to him. And he couldn't let that happen. She was loveliness incarnate; his ideal woman. She was his finest and closest friend.

A fierce need overwhelmed him. She was his. She had always been his. He had to make her see it.

"Stay with me, Sunny," he implored quietly. "Let's make this wedding real. Let's make our marriage real."

For a brief instant, he saw his own longing mirrored in her eyes. But then they clouded, and her golden brows drew together. She said in a choked whisper, "Step."

"What?" he demanded. She pushed on his arm. Tight-lipped, Ryan moved forward, and together they climbed the first stair.

The minister looked relieved. The music again built in intensity. "Why won't you marry me, Sunny?" Ryan persisted.

"Oh, Ry," she replied on a little sob, refusing to look at him. "You don't know the meaning of 'marry.'"

Frustration, and the fear that he was losing her for the final time, coursed through him as they climbed the last stair. The music reached a crescendo, then played itself out.

They found themselves in front of the minister, who bellowed into the sudden silence, "Dearly beloved, we are gathered here today to celebrate the joining in holy wedlock of Sunny Shannon and Ryan Brynfield Alexander."

He droned on, but to Sunny, the words were just a meaningless hum. This was much worse than she had feared. The man she had loved forever was asking for her hand in marriage and she couldn't accept, because marriage itself was not enough.

"Sunny." Ryan drew the back of his fingers down the curve of her jaw. "I need you." The agonized intensity of his stare filled her with pain.

The minister spluttered into silence, pulled his wire-rimmed spectacles halfway down his nose and frowned his displeasure. "Ah, I was told traditional vows..."

"Stay out of this, Preacher" came Olive's cantankerous shout. "Can't you see they're trying to talk?"

The reverend lapsed into red-faced silence, glancing awkwardly from bride to groom. But they saw only each other.

"Why do you need me, Ry?" whispered Sunny. "For sex? For business? For a child?" And though her questions couldn't have been audible to anyone but Ryan, all movement in the crowd ceased, all murmuring quieted.

She awaited his answer.

"Yes," he replied. "All that, and more. To share my life. Without you, there's no happiness. I swear before man and God, Sunny, I want you, and only you."

She was tempted to believe. So tempted. "But for how long?" she asked, sadly knowing the answer. Ryan had never believed in forever.

"Until I die," he vowed. "Probably longer."

She stared in disbelief. Then slowly, hope rose within her. A hope so clear and strong and beautiful, she was almost afraid of it.

A similar wariness lurked in his eyes. "Would you promise me the same, Sunny? Never leave me again?"

Her throat tightened. "I'll never leave you."

"Even when the going gets rough?"

She wanted to cry to think that he'd needed to ask. "Especially then. Nothing could drive me away if . . . if . . ."

And that was when reality hit. When the very heart of the matter crystalized between them.

"If . . . ?" He waited for her to go on.

A question formed on her lips. And lingered there. She didn't want to disrupt the perfection of the moment. She didn't want to ask. But, of course, she had to.

She reached out, touched his face. Gazed into his eyes, into his very soul. "Ryan, do you . . . love me?"

He drew her hand down from where it lay against his cheek and pressed it to his heart. "Yes, Sunny, I do."

Her happiness began somewhere around her heart, then spread like rays of a rising sun to every part of her.

"I do love you," he proclaimed, trying out the "L" word. Mastering it. "Do you . . . love . . . me?"

Her eyes and smile answered for her, but he waited to hear the words. She voiced them proudly. "I do."

The minister pounced at the first part of the vows he recognized. "By the power vested in me," he decreed, "I now pronounce you husband and wife."

Joyously, Ryan caught her in his arms and they joined in a pledging kiss. The music welled up as the musician flashed a famous smile from behind his keyboard and lapsed from classic into a southern, countrified rock 'n' roll version of the wedding march grand finale.

"The rings," the minister cried, abashed. "We forgot the part about the rings."

Ryan reluctantly released his bride and pulled a box from his coat pocket. Taking her left hand in his, he slipped a gold band onto her finger. "With this ring, I thee wed." The promise in his voice and eyes left no doubts in her heart.

It was a plain band, slimmer than the borrowed one she'd worn throughout the week. Very similar to the ring that had sealed their first marriage, ten long years ago.

Sunny murmured apologetically, "I didn't bring one for you. I didn't know...."

He pressed another ring into her palm. A man-sized band. Achingly familiar. She turned it to look at the engraving. *From Sunny,* it read. And the year engraved beside the words dated the band by ten years.

"Something old," he whispered.

With trembling hands and a singing heart, she slipped the band onto his finger, whispering, "Something new."

Ten years ago, the wedding ring had been a little too big. Now, it fit him perfectly.

Epilogue

THE SALE of Windsong Place was finalized the next week, but only after a major alteration in the purchase agreement.

"I don't want franchises, Lavinia," Wilbur had declared. "Too much trouble. Let's sell them all—lock, stock and barrel, and retire." Lavinia had opened her mouth, but her husband had stood his ground. "Don't argue. My mind's made up."

Ryan and Sunny Alexander honeymooned for a solid month in various tropical locales, while Mrs. Lee ran the inn with her usual efficiency. They were welcomed home to Windsong Place by their closest neighbors, Grady and Jonnie, who toasted them with glasses of sparkling cider.

Grady also presented Sunny with the oddest of all her wedding gifts—a full-length mink coat!

With considerable effort, she managed to wait until Jonnie was safely out of earshot before she described to Grady the horrible deaths those poor little animals suffered, enlightened him on the senseless butchering of their species, thanked him for the generous but misguided thought and placed the wretched thing back into his hands with a shudder.

When the newlyweds finally found themselves alone, they took time to read their mail, most of which consisted of wedding cards. Two were from perfect strangers who wrote to ask for a copy of their televised vows. One envelope that Ryan opened, however, contained not a card, but a letter.

He hesitated before opening it. After a decade, he still recognized the handwriting. His first impulse was to throw the letter away unread. To leave the past where it belonged—safely buried. But curiosity overcame his reluctance.

Dear Mr. and Mrs. Ryan Alexander,
I saw your wedding on television, and I'm happy to admit you've proved me wrong. I thought your love would ruin your lives, as my first love almost ruined mine. It took years for me, Ryan, to place the blame where it belonged—not on my wife, your mother, but on myself. I was not a good husband to her, or a good father to you.

I'm thankful we've both been given a second chance. I've recently remarried, and have come to know the gentler side of love. I never would have forgiven myself if I had deprived you of the same.

I was bidding on Windsong Place to right another wrong. If I had won it, I would have deeded it over to you. The house is yours, by right. And by your enviable ability, Ryan, to attain any goal you set your sights on. You've done me proud, son.

Sunny, I ask your forgiveness. Not many people would have walked away from the money I once offered you. You have a rare strength, the kind that could bring even the strongest man to his knees. Ten years ago, that strength scared me. What I didn't understand was the nature of your love. I'd be honored to call you daughter.

My sincerest congratulations on your marriage. Can you someday find room in your hearts for a father?

Love,
Edgar Rockwell Alexander III

And though hell never did freeze over, they found ample room, not only in their hearts, but in the finest guest quarters of Windsong Place.

BRIDE'S
BAY RESORT

UNLOCK THE DOOR TO GREAT ROMANCE AT BRIDE'S BAY RESORT

Join Harlequin's new across-the-lines series, set in an exclusive hotel on an island off the coast of South Carolina.

Seven of your favorite authors will bring you exciting stories about fascinating heroes and heroines discovering love at Bride's Bay Resort.

Look for these fabulous stories coming to a store near you beginning in January 1996.

Harlequin American Romance #613 in January
Matchmaking Baby by Cathy Gillen Thacker

Harlequin Presents #1794 in February
Indiscretions by Robyn Donald

Harlequin Intrigue #362 in March
Love and Lies by Dawn Stewardson

Harlequin Romance #3404 in April
Make Believe Engagement by Day Leclaire

Harlequin Temptation #588 in May
Stranger in the Night by Roseanne Williams

Harlequin Superromance #695 in June
Married to a Stranger by Connie Bennett

Harlequin Historicals #324 in July
Dulcie's Gift by Ruth Langan

Visit Bride's Bay Resort each month wherever Harlequin books are sold.

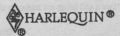

HARLEQUIN®

BBAYG

Take 4 bestselling love stories FREE

Plus get a FREE surprise gift!

HARLEQUIN® *Temptation*

THE WRONG BED

The Wrong Bed? The Wrong Twin?
The Ultimate Temptation

It was ten years since Emily Rose had seen "Chigger" Callister, but he'd grown up to be sheriff of Bluster County and a magnificent specimen of manhood, just as she'd pictured him in her bedtime fantasies. She couldn't quite pin down his personality, though. She never knew which Callister she was going to see.

It was almost as if there were two of him.

Don't miss:

#591 TWIN BEDS
Regan Forest

Available in June wherever Harlequin books are sold.

What do women really want to know?

Trust the world's largest publisher of
women's fiction to tell you.

HARLEQUIN ULTIMATE GUIDES™

I CAN FIX THAT

A Guide For Women
Who Want To Do It Themselves

This is the only guide a self-reliant
woman will ever need to deal
with those pesky items that
break, wear out or just don't work
anymore. Chock-full of friendly
advice and straightforward,
step-by-step solutions to the
trials of everyday life in our
gadget-oriented world! So, don't
just sit there wondering how to
fix the VCR—run to your
nearest bookstore for your copy now!

Available this May, at your favorite retail outlet.

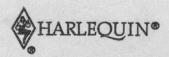

HARLEQUIN®

FIX

Bestselling authors

ELAINE COFFMAN
RUTH LANGAN
and
MARY McBRIDE

Together in one fabulous collection!

**Available in June wherever Harlequin
books are sold.**

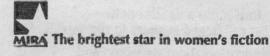

You're About to Become a *Privileged Woman*

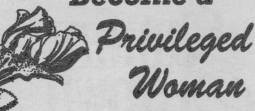

Reap the rewards of fabulous free gifts and benefits with proofs-of-purchase from Harlequin and Silhouette books

Pages & Privileges™

It's our way of thanking you for buying our books at your favorite retail stores.

PROOF OF PURCHASE

HT-PP137

Offer expires October 31, 1996

Pages & Privileges™

Harlequin and Silhouette— the most privileged readers in the world!

For more information about Harlequin and Silhouette's PAGES & PRIVILEGES program call the Pages & Privileges Benefits Desk: 1-503-794-2499

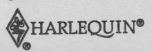

HARLEQUIN®

HT-PP137